BITTER
MAREMMA

BITTER MAREMMA

A LEAH CONTARINI MYSTERY

LIBI SIPORIN

LEVEL
BEST BOOKS

DISCLAIMER:

This is a work of fiction. The characters and their names, the names of places, and the incidents are products of the author's imagination. Any resemblance to actual events, locales, organizations, or persons, living or dead, is coincidental.

That said, the Befanata is a real and rooted celebration that takes place on the eve of Epiphany. The particular Befanata I describe in this book is fictional, a product of my imagination. The vie cave are actual trails, but the trail I describe in this book is fictional. The evil acts and people described in this book are entirely fictional.

This book was previously published under a different name in a different form.

Second edition

ISBN: 978-1-68512-007-8

Cover art by Level Best Designs

This book was professionally typeset on Reedsy.
Find out more at reedsy.com

To Jerry and Joe, and to the memory of Mary and Dana

Praise for Libi Siporin's Mysteries

"I love Libi Siporin's writing; her words are wise and I always like her perspective. She captures the interest of the reader; her characters are real. I want to reach out and touch them. I want to walk along the streets with them. I have been to Italy many times, most recently to Firenze and Venezia, so I can picture the areas. And I can picture her characters as they interact with each other. I'm looking forward to reading more." – Pamela Lazarus

"Libi Siporin has the voice of a storyteller; she captures her reader as she spins her tale, and she holds that reader in her spell. Her skill and art as a poet come through in her fiction writing; there is a certain gentle, yet compelling poetic voice to her tale of mystery. One can picture her characters with ease; they are distinct from one another, and they are memorable. She has a strong sense of setting; she 'paints' her scenes with clarity and depth." – Roz Stein

Chapter One

Leah Contarini bumped down the steps to the basement, ignored the dirty laundry on the floor next to the washing machine, and opened the door to her husband's office. When he looked up, she smiled and curled her index finger at him.

"A glass or two of wine? Sun's down. Canyon breeze up. Chips and salsa on the balcony?"

Nick smiled. His wife was funny—and unpredictable. When did they ever have chips and salsa on the balcony?

"Can't do it. If I drink wine now, I'll be blotto the rest of the evening."

"Half a glass. Come on. You need to prepare for Tuscany."

"We're not there yet."

"Half a glass…"

She whined like a six-year-old, twisting her shoulders, rolling her eyes.

He laughed.

"I could have sworn you said a glass or two."

She had, but pretended not to have.

"Just half a glass, come on, and then you can work while I fix dinner."

She did a little dance of good-willed impatience.

"After we'll eat, read, and later you can tell me about the sabbatical proposal, and I'll tell you about the article I'm going to write on Scansansiano while we're there."

He held out his arms to her. She moved into them, and he buried his face in her stomach.

"I like the plan."

"Good!"

"But…"

He dropped his arms. They both turned to stare at the computer screen.

"I'm tired of this proposal. You'd think I'd proved myself enough already without having to go through it all again. It takes so much time."

Her arm draped around his shoulder, she kissed him on the head.

"Mornings are wiser than evenings. Finish up while I fix dinner, then let it go for today. I'm done with the article for *Traveling!* so in the morning I can go over what you've already written while you continue with the last part, and when I'm finished, we'll trade. Okay?"

"Okay."

She kissed him again.

Chapter Two

Nick paced the small living room of the apartment he and Leah had rented in Scansansiano, not far from Siena. He was trying to nail down his feelings. They'd had an argument that morning about the photos for Leah's article, photos he was supposed to take.

Nick could almost admit, at least to himself, he'd forgotten Leah expected him to take the photos that morning. But today was his preparation for the approaching evening, his actual fieldwork on the *Befanata*, the Epiphany celebration he hoped would be the basis for a new book and tenure. Had she so easily forgotten that? After all, he'd been studying and researching for years, but now, ready as he was and waiting for evening, he still felt restless and agitated. Was that so surprising?

They'd gone back and forth. Leah insisted he had promised, was well-prepared, and had reneged on his promise only out of nervousness. She, don't forget, needed to finish the photos. Her work was important too.

Of course. He knew that. He did support her work, and he knew he was the better photographer, but he needed to test the tape recorder and read through a few things.

After their daughter, Sara, had called and Leah had given up arguing and stalked out the door, Nick realized Leah had been right. He was prepared, overprepared, and walking with her on the trails would have been a good way to dispel his anxiety.

Still, he'd stubbornly refused to go with her.

Now he felt concerned, and she was off alone on the *vie cave*, the deep trails bounded by steep walls of tufa that snaked through the forests surrounding town.

Their argument echoed other arguments they'd had and recalled other incidents. Nick understood the article wasn't the only concern, although it was a significant one.

A woman of exhilarating enthusiasm and boundless energy, Leah had a stubborn, dark side that too often landed her in trouble. Wily, strong, but impetuous, she had gotten entangled in more incidents than he cared to count. Climbing in the Canadian Rockies with an inept guide who didn't know the route, she had barely saved herself on an overhang, she had escaped death by a hair's breadth in a horseback-riding accident in Tajikistan, and she eluded a terrorist attack in West Africa by hiding in a pile of refuse. There was something about her. Without looking for trouble, she never seemed to be more than a day or two away from it.

Nick lay on the couch, closed his eyes, opened them, rose, and wandered into the bathroom, where he bent his tall frame to stare at himself in the mirror and run his fingers vigorously through his wavy, dark blond hair. How had he managed to get into this kind of stand-off with Leah yet again?

Leah had once told him his green eyes held a perpetually inquisitive look, as if not only Leah, but life itself, puzzled him. He questioned and analyzed everything. The world, particularly the people in it, were curious enough for him to spend a lifetime of study.

Thinking of Leah's impatience with his habit of questioning minute details, he uttered a little laugh and pulled at his hair again. He had begun this habitual gesture of tugging at his hair in the tumultuous first years of he and Leah's too-early marriage. Those years, Leah traveled incessantly and got into trouble; he was overwhelmed with the demands of graduate school and the impending burden of a dissertation; Sara, just a baby, woke several times at night; and even with graduate school over, they were compelled to move from city to city, from one interim job to another. After the short-lived joy of finally receiving a tenure track position, came the crushing news of early-stage colon cancer.

"I'll be bald either way," he muttered to his reflection. "If the cancer comes back, I'll lose my hair; if I live a while longer, I'll pull it out."

He laughed.

A circus, a wonderful circus.

Or anyway it would have been without the cancer.

He deflected the thought. Still in hospital, he had decided to follow his goal, to get on with life. Whatever was going to happen would happen.

He made a face at himself and returned to the kitchen.

At the small wooden table that doubled as a desk, he straightened the tape recorder, checked the microphone, and picked up his notes, thinking what a godsend the research grant had been.

Setting the notes down again, he moved to the window and looked out on the river below, remembering how he heard of the Befanata.

It was years earlier, late December. He and Leah were on one of their rare vacations and had stopped for lunch in Scansansiano on their way to Rome. Two couples at the table next to them were talking about the local Befanata. Epiphany was approaching, and one of the men planned to participate. He would, he told them, travel through the countryside with the troupe of musicians and singers led by the *Befana*, a kindly old witch; the *Befano*, her husband; and the *figlia di maritare*, their daughter to marry off.

With the folklorist's curiosity, Nick had leaned closer to eavesdrop. The couples laughed at his blatant attempts to hide the fact he was snooping and with generous goodwill invited him and Leah to join them. Nick reciprocated with an after-dinner offer of grappa and coffee.

The couples explained that the Befanata was a local celebration that took place on the eve of Epiphany, a kind of mumming similar to a custom in England and Ireland. A group of mainly young people, usually cross-dressed in costume, went from house to house through the countryside, singing the Befana song and receiving food and drink in return. The songs and the visits continued until dawn.

By the time Nick and Leah rose to leave the restaurant that day, Nick was bursting with dozens of questions and had determined his next sabbatical project.

It had been a long road from the lively conversation in Ristorante da Giorgio to Nick's nervous pacing that day in the apartment above the Tuscan forests. There had been years of teaching, years of research in English and Italian, countless phone calls with requests for material from Italian archives—some fulfilled, some refused—help from some librarians, suspicion from others. He had corresponded with Italian friends, read anything about the Befanata he could find, and he and Leah had worked hard to develop and polish their Italian.

Finally, the grant and the approaching evening of the actual event. With luck he hadn't expected, Nick had been invited to join one of the several Befanata groups of musicians, singers, and their followers, who would gather in preparation for visits to local farmsteads. With accordions, guitars, mandolins, fiddles, and perhaps a saxophone or trumpet, they would stop at the houses they had chosen, park their cars, and descend to walk to the house, playing and singing traditional songs, all led by the costumed characters of the kindly witch, her husband, and the daughter.

Nick imagined earlier times when the troupes walked the whole night, strolling from farmhouse to farmhouse with their company of musicians and singers. This night they would drive. He imagined the company of singers and musicians packed tightly together in cars, laughing, discussing who to visit next.

Thinking about it, excitement overwhelmed his normal reserve, and he burst into the first lines of the traditional Befanata song, sung as the group approached and entered each house.

> Good evening to you in the house.
> Tonight is Epiphany,
> And in the name of Maria
> We come to greet you...

Embarrassed by his own outburst, he stopped abruptly.

Invited into the house, the Befana and the Befano would ask the master and mistress of the house to dance, while the musicians played and the others watched. Following the lead of the Befana and Befano, family members, friends, and the Befanata troupe would all began to dance, switching partners, laughing, stopping now and then to eat and drink from the heavily laden tables of savories, sweets, wine, and grappa provided by the hosts.

Nick stood and paced, thankful for the friends who had invited him for the evening, thankful for the possibility of studying an ancient custom that continued to thrive. His choices at university had led him to folklore, exactly where he felt he was supposed to be. Discoveries of traditional artists, of customs seemingly simple, but profoundly informative of human behavior, excited him.

What would the Befanata tell him about the communities that practice it? What would the communities lose if the custom faded away? How was the Befanata of Scansansiano different from other regions?

Niggling at the edge of his excitement was the vision of Leah on the vie cave. He couldn't shake the worry, exacerbated by the argument over the photos.

Had he actually promised it would be today?

He didn't want to think about her alone on the trail; he wanted to think about his own work. She should have understood.

On the Go & Free. He grunted. The name of the magazine described her perfectly. It was no wonder they continued to ask her to write for them. She was willing to go anywhere, and had, and was ready to write about anything. Her independence irked him, angered him, and made him proud. Siberian Husky. Or rock chuck in the hills skittering from boulder to boulder. Fox, scampering, sniffing here and there as it crossed a meadow. She was all of them.

He returned to the table to test his tape recorder, then stood again and walked back to the windows.

The little apartment they had rented just below Piazza Portarini was usually a refuge for him. Their two rooms hung above the fork of the Bieta and Lavini rivers. With a glance out the window, he could see for miles across forests, green fields, and meadows toward San Giorgio and Bareno, other originally Etruscan villages.

Today the apartment was no retreat. He couldn't concentrate. He was cold. He was excited. He was thinking about Leah, wondering about Sara. The whir of family and work.

He punched the pellet stove up a notch, impatient at the minutes it would take to kick in. He put the kettle on for tea, staring at the floor until the water fumed at the spout. With a sharp knife, he sliced a lemon, squeezed the tart juice into the cup as the tea steeped, added a full tablespoon of the local thick-brown honey, his weakness, and carried the cup to the table.

Publishing a book on the Befanata promised a raise. With the book finished and out, he could continue research on other aspects of Italian culture.

Leah. He thought of her bright green eyes, thought of her on the vie cave trying for the best shots with her less than perfect camera.

What the hell is wrong with me!

Abandoning the cup of tea steaming on the wooden table, Nick grabbed his jacket from the hook by the door, snatched his camera, and headed down the mottled stone steps toward the dark trails.

Chapter Three

Leah pushed upward along the ancient trail, Via Cava San Raffaello. She was thinking of a line from Tolstoy: "I wanted movement... danger..."

Unaware how soon both desires would be granted, Leah forged ahead with a determined, look on her face.

Leah was not a beautiful woman, but her illimitable energy and eager aspect gave her lanky body, unruly black-as-a-deep-stream curls, and flashing smile an attractive quality that went beyond the physical. Wrapped in an aura of excitement, Leah remained oblivious to her own magnetism. Her curiosity was not for the mirror, but for the world that lay in front of her restless green eyes. At the moment, that world meant the thirty-meter walls of tufa rising on either side of her. These vertical faces of rock hugged the trail so closely she could spread her arms and touch both sides of the dank stone, shaded now from the first light of morning by overhanging sessile and holm oak.

An early January chill seeped under Leah's jacket, encircled her narrow waist, and ran down her arms. Every hike on the vie cave enlivened her. Hewn from solid tufa over 2500 years before, the trails promised mystery and challenge, just what Leah liked.

Nick and Sara teased Leah calling her a Siberian Husky, cousin to the wolf, great on long hikes and trail runs, in love with the cold, able to fend for herself, curious about every cave, every stone.

But too independent.

The analogy worked in two ways. Her energy and excitement were both a curse and a blessing. She had struggled most of her life with a chemistry that, like a hand at her back, pushed her forward, usually into trouble. She refused medication. Even with the episodes of turbulence that fell in her path and scattered behind her, she liked being who she was, liked the energy.

"Pills make me dull-headed," she countered, "I'll stick with motion."

Nick, Sara, and a few friends were the only ones who knew this destructively impetuous and stubborn underbelly of Leah's character, yet still loved her with full hearts. For Leah, relationships other than these few were a walk on a tightrope, an attempt to maintain balance between her inner self and a social life.

The exertion of the upward ascent cleansed Leah of the frustration she felt when she left the apartment. Weeks earlier, Nick had mentioned that if he had time, he would take photos for her article. She had ignored the "if" and had taken his tentative commitment as a promise.

So, in the dark of that early morning, she shook his shoulder to wake him. He rolled over, pulled the covers over his head, and mumbled, "Not this morning, Leah. I need to get ready for tonight."

Nettled by his response, she contended that he had promised. She had gotten angry, and they argued until she stalked to the door. Then, just at the moment she stepped into the dark morning, the phone on the counter exploded in an earsplitting jangle loud enough to wake the neighbors down the hill.

Leah burst back into the apartment. The noise rattled her. She made an irritated swipe of her fist and grabbed the phone from its little dance on the counter.

Sara and Jonathan had changed wedding plans, again. More than merely change plans, they had decided to postpone the whole event. Leah envisioned the dozens of long-distance phone calls it would take to right the situation.

Nick had barreled out of the bedroom to stand next to Leah.

When Leah hung up, he asked, "What is it? Is she okay?"

"They're postponing the wedding."

"Again!"

Leah nodded.

"But the caterers, hotel rooms…that garden on the coast."

Leah nodded.

"How come you're so calm?" Nick asked.

She laughed and made a face. "Aren't I usually?"

The look of dismay on his face reminded her of nights in the hospital after his last surgery, when she bent to hug him goodnight before she settled in the recliner next to the bed. They had labored through a decade of pain and tension to arrive at the choice of laughter over logistics. But that morning, both of them tender from the argument, they could not make it over the bridge of frustration with each other, and she left.

Breathing rhythmically, Leah continued upward, her spirit lightening, like a leaf wafted by the breeze. Her anger had faded.

A rock shifted above her. She stopped, looked up, and listened.

The branches of a large holm oak trembled in the breeze, and vines dangling from the edges at the top of the sheer wall fluttered like the skirt of a dancer. A breath of air meandered through the spiked ferns, springing like fingers from the cracks in the rocks.

Squirrel?

The breeze pirouetted through the brush above her. She expelled a long breath and smiled. Sara had some reason for the sudden change of plans, and that reason would become known. Their beautiful, stubborn daughter had something in mind and would find her way, marriage whenever, or not at all.

A few dark curls slipped from beneath Leah's navy wool hat. She reached to tuck them in, then started upward once again humming "Seven Golden Daffodils," a song a friend used to sing long ago. The memory of her friend brought a wave of nostalgia. It seemed she had inevitably lost people she cared about, by circumstances or by her own failures, and she had accepted that at least as long as there is life and mind nothing can erase memories or negate enduring love.

The morning mist cooled Leah's face. She hummed into the silence, aware of the rough path below her feet, the wet stone walls at her side. She anticipated with joy the sight of the fields of grapes vines and the thousand green hills of Tuscany that would spread around her when she reached the top.

Leah rounded a curve. On both sides of the trail, gaping mouths of broad, low-ceilinged caverns opened into what had been Etruscan burial caves, but were now empty except for the wide stone benches and broad shelves carved into the tufa walls. These had been the benches where family members sat next to the pottery urns, the ashes of their loved ones. Long since robbed of the stucco reliefs, carved household items, festive urns or sarcophagi, the caves were now bare of all but dust and a lingering musty smell.

Leah could imagine the joyous funerary rites that would have taken place in the caves: festive occasions with dancing and dining, in the belief a bright party with elaborately decorated gifts would make the passage to the next world a happy one and would foretell pleasure and comfort for the dead.

And maybe prevent the deceased from coming back to torment the living, Leah thought.

The caves acted as a test. After Nick's diagnosis in the early years of their marriage, Leah stubbornly pushed herself, challenged herself. In breaks from the hospital and care of Sara, she hiked the most difficult trails, rode her bike to exhaustion. Fear had wormed its way into her body, and since Nick had been in remission, she had continued to ignite herself by turning to the outdoors, walking alone, enticing danger. Exercise had become a superstition: if she faced the world alone, walked fast enough, sweat enough, wore herself to exhaustion, she could skirt a recurrence of Nick's cancer, avert his death. If she entered the caves, which intimidated her, she could prevent death and tame her own cascade of emotions, which had put her in debt to everyone she had ever loved. She would plunge into each day, each situation, forcing life to give itself to her, and by sympathetic magic, to Nick.

Fall down seven, get up eight. Mixing magic with belief, she let the biblical injunction from Proverbs become her model, a mantra to counteract fear, resist worry, ward off return of the cancer.

She walked into the first of the caves and tasted what she imagined to be the fetid, remnant odor of a dead Etruscan. The smell and aura elicited fantasies, layers of stories that pervaded the empty air. Leah thought of all the lives that had walked these trails: women in their flowing robes, workmen who had patiently chipped the pathways and the caverns out of this warren of volcanic tufa gorges. The curved walls of the cave still showed the embedded, sweeping pattern of the double-edged tool of the laborers.

Leah had the uncanny sense that other lives were being lived at the edge of her peripheral vision. What were their dances? The sound of their music? Most of all, what of their immanent polytheism. What messages did they receive from the flight of birds, the sounds of thunder, or the jagged arrows of lightning? She might understand, she thought, a religion with such a close connection to these facets of the natural world.

Leah sat on the ledge carved from the wall of the cave, where the family would have sat during funerary rites, and let herself be blanketed by lives and stories that had been lived and now hovered at the edge of her vision.

These encounters with the caves and solitary hikes along the trails, where death lingered, rekindled the woman that had been temporarily vanquished by watching the suffering of the man she loved. Here she found again that Siberian Husky Nick had loved from the beginning, a strong woman, but perhaps not strong enough to keep her recklessness or the jaws of the world at bay.

Back on the trail, strands of Leah's hair fell loose again. She stopped, pulled her hat from her head, tossed her long black curls out of her face, and clasping her hair at the nape of her neck, tucked the thick mass of curls back under her stocking cap. Shaking her head to make sure the cap was tight, she continued upward, wishing she had thought to bring a flask of Brunello di Montalcino to warm her.

Ascending, Leah placed her feet carefully at the lip of each depression in the rough path. Thousands of men's and women's steps and donkey's hooves had pockmarked the stones beneath her feet. For centuries, the surefooted burros, led by their owners, had been carrying wood and produce up and down, from the level fields above, down to the valley below, across the river, and up to the town, then back along the same route.

Nearing the top of the ridge, Leah stepped through a break in the trail wall onto a broad overhang of rock. There, centuries before, some skilled stoneworker had chiseled and chipped the giant boulder to form a flat floor, a throne with wide armrests, and a curved bench facing the lip of the boulder.

She stared out at the view before her. On the far side of the gorge, the twists and turns of the river lay like a silver bracelet on the land. Above the river, a field of radiant green winter-wheat spread like a silk scarf. The thread of another via cava curved through the field, stretching upward to a meadow laying along the crest of the high tableland. A flock of sheep grazed there, in the new dawn, and after the previous night's downpour the air was crystalline, the sky a pure cerulean with frothy white clouds wafting toward the northeast.

She looked downward. Below her, the steep slope was covered with thick forest and an entangled mass of brush and bamboo breaks. The tips of the slender trees jutted like spikes skyward.

Leah edged toward the unfenced lip of the rock, remembering her father's fear of heights. A master carpenter, he had often worked on the roofs of the houses he built, but he had never lost his fear of high places. Leah felt an atavistic jolt of panic along her limbs, as if she carried his spirit with her.

Craning her neck, she peered downward at the forest and underbrush that covered the steep descent to the river. The foliage glistened from the night's rain. She stepped back, pulled her small pack to the front, and switched out her macro lens for her zoom. The early morning light cast shadows, but the effect pleased her, and she snapped several photos, aware she would need to take more when the sun had risen higher in the sky.

Leah turned to see the whole of the landscape. Below her, she spied another flat outcrop along a narrow trail that twisted off and downward from the way she had come. She realized from that lower outcrop she could get an impressive shot of the table rock on which she was standing. It would perfectly demonstrate the sheer drop and the thick forests of what had been one of the centers of Etruscan civilization, and it would make clear for the readers how hidden the vie cave were to the casual eye. She imagined a photo of the wooded side of the gorge, with an overlay red line to trace at least one of the trails.

Leaving the table rock, Leah followed the narrow trail downward, squeezed through a hole between two bushes, and stepped onto the rock she had seen from above. She pulled a soft cloth from her pocket, wiped her lens, and raised her camera.

The timing was perfect for murder.

While Leah had adjusted the camera, two figures stepped onto the table rock above, arguing. One, wearing dark clothing and a brimmed hat, was pushing the other in the chest. The second, a large man dressed in the blue overalls of a laborer, stumbled backward toward the edge of the rock, righting himself just in time."

Leah heard him laugh nervously and shout, "Hey, be careful."

She had raised her camera and held it steady on the two men. Having figures in the photo would make a better picture, if they would just stand still for a second.

At the moment she clicked the shutter, the shorter figure stepped forward with a quick gesture of both hands and shoved the larger man in the chest.

Later, Leah would dream of the man catapulting into the air, transformed to a rag doll, screaming, arms flaying for purchase as he fell through the vast expanse of emptiness toward the steep forest floor.

In the next second, Leah saw the other one turn to scan the brush and outcrops. Seeing her, he froze, pointed, and jumped down onto the smaller trail.

He was coming for her.

Chapter Four

Leah bounded pell-mell down the rock trail. Seeing an opening onto the main trail, she leapt through and hurdled downward, her camera banging against her body. Every step her foot slipped on loose rocks. She clenched her toes for purchase, threw out her hands to keep balance, and sucked air. In the panic of flight, she felt as if she were in a dream of impotence, like the dreams of her childhood: a wild boar was chasing her. She had only to reach the fence, but weighted by terror, her legs dragged, heavy as stone, and she moved in an excruciatingly slow motion, the breath of the boar at her neck.

Skidding along the wet trail, she smacked her palms against the rock wall to steady herself as she flew past and strained to discern between the sounds of her own labored breathing and the pounding footsteps and heavy gasps of the killer.

Rounding a curve in the trail she saw that the rock walls opened on a grassy field perched above the gorge. A smudged sign at the edge of the opening read: NECROPOLIS, ETRUSCAN BURIAL GROUNDS.

In the lucidity of terror, she spotted impressions in the fresh earth at the bottom of the sign and recognized the snout marks of *cinghiali*, the tusked boars that lived in these thick woods, rooting, feeding off acorns of the holm oak.

Terror on terror, she felt a sudden need to vomit, but swallowed hard, refusing to give way to the impulse. There could be a drift of boars nearby, but there was no choice. Lurching headlong through the opening in the tufa wall, she broke into the field only a few steps from two picnic tables set on a patch of grass. To the side, a rickety wooden fence surrounded three deep dromoi, sunken passages that led into subterranean burial caves.

Hurtling over the fence, she saw the first dromos was filled with murky water that reached three feet up the wall of the sloped entryway. She leapt to the next. The twisted arms of a wild raspberry bush made an impassable wall across the opening.

The third dromos was dry. Leah ducked under the wooden railing and dropped into the narrow mouth of the cave. Staring into the black maw, she faltered, hesitating, until the sound of a rock tumbling on the pathway urged her forward. She plunged into darkness.

Crazy with fear and need of light, Leah grabbed at her camera and clicked on the tiny screen. In the faint glow, she made out a low ledge with a wide, deep hole beneath it. Her light faded. She dropped to her knees and scrambled toward the opening, banging her shoulder against the ledge before she fell flat and scooted into the tight space, darker than the dark of the cave.

The must of death was strong. Again, she gagged. Grabbing her hat off her head, she held it tightly over her mouth to muffle the sound, breathing through her nose. The hat stifled her breath. She swallowed her gorge to keep from vomiting outright and pushed herself further in until she lay flat against the back of the little alcove she hoped would save her.

Pulling air through the loose weave of her hat, Leah forced her breathing to slow. The cave went silent.

Then, footsteps. Heavy bursts of breath.

Chapter Five

Panting like a dog, the killer gasped in an agonized rhythm that echoed in Leah's ears. In a macabre counterpoint to his ragged breathing, he prodded the floor and crevices of the cave with a long stick. The thin, brittle wood rasped against the tufa and jittered along the pocked walls. With each intake of breath, Leah smelled the dust raised as the stick swept to and fro, tapping with a maddening beat.

The cave walls amplified the sound. Leah squeezed her eyes and hunched her shoulders to dampen the deafening judder of breathing and stick. She crammed her hat hard against her mouth, stifling the thunder of her own breath, and tilted her chin downward, attempting to arrest the light-headed sensation she felt from drawing air through her hat. Huddled in a fetal position, her chest rose and fell like the jabs of a knife, and her stomach muscles worked against her legs, against her pounding heart.

Leah sensed the tapping closer with each step. It was Nick's death she had feared, but in the comedy of reality, she was facing not his death, but her own.

She felt a crazy urge to laugh, to laugh aloud at the absurdity of it all, the impossibility of the coincidence of her photo. Within minutes she would be dead, with no time to prepare, no time to say goodbye.

She struggled against a strange and powerful impatience. Death was here, in front of her. She ached to stand, to face the dark, to fight. She craved the relief of combat, a means to stop the horrible rhythm of breath and the panic of the tapping stick, even if it meant death would arrive a few minutes earlier.

Allured beyond resistance, Leah scrambled from under the ledge and pushed herself to her feet screaming, screeching in the deafening wild sounds of a cornered animal.

The dark figure before her stood immobile, but in the next instant raised an arm to strike. Leah sprang to the side, not fast enough.

Chapter Six

When the phone shrilled, Lieutenant Cavour was sitting at his desk in the police station staring out the window. He had passed a restless night thinking about Bibiana, his sister in Sardinia. Her fiancé, a wealthy distant relation, had broken off his engagement to Bibiana, and his mother feared Bibiana might hurt herself.

Contrary to their mother's imaginings, Lieutenant Cavour knew Bibiana was overjoyed. She had been badgered into the marriage. Led by Bachisio, a family friend who had talked ceaselessly of the relative's wealth and the comfort and security it would bring Bibiana and the whole family, their father had been convinced. He settled the match and foolishly promised once the wedding took place, he would give his friend Bachisio a goodly sum of money for arranging the match.

When "Uncle" Arrafiele, a short, balding, rotund little man who ran a fabric shop, heard of the proposal he was euphoric. A widower of forty-six, he had fawned over Bibiana since she had turned sixteen. She was his fantasy. He spent long, lonely nights dreaming of Bibiana's dark-eyed beauty and the male heirs he would take great pleasure in siring on his marriage bed.

The news that Uncle Arrafiele had broken the engagement puzzled the Lieutenant. Arrafiele was one of those men never content with what he had, and one who would never be content until he got what he wanted. Given his greedy desires for Bibiana, and even her small dowry, his lust had become plain to everyone in the village. So why had he broken the engagement?

Through a friend, the Lieutenant learned that in his zeal for Bibiana's beauty and overanxious for the wedding night, still months away, Uncle

Arrafiele had behaved in a boorish manner to his sister when they had been left alone, sitting on the couch in the living room. In response to Arrafiele's coarse behavior, Bibiana had socked him, one direct blow to the eye and another to parts unmentionable. Her blows gave lie to her ostensibly delicate physical attributes, and when she promised him more of the same if he didn't leave, he rushed from the room, shouting it was all over.

The Lieutenant knew Uncle Arrafiele would come back. Bibiana was too beautiful to resist. The Lieutenant was also convinced Uncle Arrafiele would stay holed up in his shop for a few weeks, contemplating a different version of what he had imagined for the wedding night, sweating bullets to figure a way to make his original dream a reality. The Lieutenant hoped this delay would give him time to get to Sardinia and help his sister convince their parents the match was not a good one.

Having grown up with his sister and being fully aware of her strength from the time they had wrestled as children, the Lieutenant laughed to himself over Arrafiele's predicament.

At the same time, he worried for Bibiana. She was suffering at the hands of their parents. He could imagine the angry shouts and stern admonishments from their father and the endless whiny exhortations of their mother. He needed to get home for at least a week.

While the Lieutenant mused, the phone continued to ring. Seeing the caller refused to give up, the Lieutenant gave in and lifted the phone off its cradle.

"Pronto, Cavour here."

"Good morning, Lieutenant. Leonardo Antonini.

"Good morning, Leonardo! It's been too long. How are you?"

"Fine, thanks. You?"

"A little bored. Nothing's happening. How can I help you?"

"I'd like to bring my gun into town and walk down the trail by the river to meet friends for a few hours hunting."

"Of course, bring it along. You're one of the few who always take care to apply for permission to transport their guns. I know I can trust you to store it properly in the car. Stop on your way home, will you?"

"I will. It'd be a pleasure to see you."

"I wish I could join you. I'm bored to death."

"Crime never sleeps, Lieutenant. You'll end up wishing you had nothing to do."

The Lieutenant laughed. "Don't curse me, Leonardo."

Chapter Seven

The faint, high pitch of a whistle curled into the opening of the cave. Leah gasped and opened her eyes without moving. It was the sound of the whistle Leah had given Nick when they were on vacation in Cascais.

Why was Nick blowing his whistle? Where was he? And where am I?

Her head throbbed. It was dark, except for a light some yards away, a light blocked by a human form that stood riveted in place.

The sound of the whistle stopped, and the air of the cave, the darkness, trembled with a thick, hesitant silence. What was happening?

Leah lifted her hand to touch the side of her head. Her hair felt wet, sticky. Nick's whistle sounded again.

Leah pawed at her clothing, searching for the chain around her neck, for the whistle Nick had given her in return for her gift. Nauseated, shaking, she clutched the small silver whistle in hand, fumbling to bring it to her mouth.

The high pitch from outside sounded again, closer than before.

She heard a muttered curse and watched as the form turned, ran into full light, and disappeared.

Leah brought her whistle to her lips and blew three short bursts, three long bursts, and three short bursts, again, and then again, as she staggered to her feet and stumbled toward the opening of the cave.

Chapter Eight

"What are you doing?"

From the top of the dromos, Nick rushed down toward her. Leah stepped forward, stopped, tilted her head to the side, and vomited in the dust. Staring at Nick, she prodded the half-digested food away from her face with the back of her hand.

"Thank God you're okay." She spoke with an odd slur, then lurched toward him, trembling. "Did you see him?"

"See who? What's going on? What happened, Leah?"

He pulled her to his chest and stroked her hair.

"What's this?" He raised his hand and looked at it. "Leah! You're bleeding!"

"We're not safe!" She took his hand and tugged him toward the trail.

Nick resisted. "What are you talking about? Tell me what's happening!"

"Forget about the blood. A murder. I saw a murder. I took a picture of it. It was a coincidence; I wanted the landscape. Somebody shoved a man off the table rock, you know the one? With the seats? And the guy toppled over the edge, like a doll, Nick. He grabbed at the air and kept screaming. It happened just as I pressed the shutter release. I think I have a picture of it. He saw me and chased me, and I was hiding, but he was here. He hit me with a stick or a rock or something."

Nick held her at arm's length, squeezing her shoulders hard. Her fear infected him, and he raised his voice.

"Slow down, Leah. Damn it! Look at me. Look me in the eyes. *Who* was here?"

He put his palms to her cheeks and forced her to look at him. "Do you mean in the cave? Take a deep breath and look at me! You're bleeding; we've got to get you to the doctor."

"It's just a scratch! Listen, please! I saw a murder."

He wiped his hand over her wound; she slapped him away.

"Okay. You saw someone push a guy off the cliff at table rock?"

"It's what I told you!" She wrenched her arm from his grasp and shoved the camera toward him. "Look!"

Nick turned on the camera and pressed the review button. A photo of the cave floor appeared on the screen. "Not that one! That's the one I took to get light. Go back!"

Nick pressed the return and a picture of the murder flashed onto the monitor.

"My God! It looks like Giulio."

"Let me see." Leah took the camera.

"I'm certain it's him," Nick said, "He's the guy who runs the knickknack shop with Silvio, just off the piazza. You know him. His face isn't clear, but he always wears those blue coveralls. The other one's too dark to tell. Do you think the other one recognized you?"

"I don't think so. He would have said my name in the cave, and I had my hair tucked up in my cap, and I'm wearing the coat I bought here, so I could have seemed Italian."

"Good God, Leah. How do you do it! How do you get into these messes, and today of all days?"

"I'm sorry! How could I know I'd see a murder?"

"Okay. Okay. At least we can identify Giulio. Was there anything about the other one?"

"There was something glistening on his head, part of the hat, but I was too far away to tell what it was, or to see faces, and you can see by the photo there were shadows—that early morning light."

"What else?"

"I don't know! Stop asking! We need to get out of here and get to Lieutenant Cavour."

"Okay, but first give me your hat and coat. Have you got a scarf?"

"Why?"

"We can't let anyone see you in this hat and coat."

He balled them together and stuck them in the little pack he carried, then took off his jacket and held it for her. She put it on, tied the scarf over her head, and they stepped through the opening onto the trail to begin the descent.

Chapter Nine

In town, Leah and Nick skirted the piazza and made their way back to the apartment to dress the laceration.

"It must have been a rock, an edge of some sort anyway," Nick said when he pulled back her hair to study the gash. "It's sliced, not blunt force."

"Doesn't matter which one. I feel ok. Let's get to the Lieutenant."

The police station was locked. A note on the door said Cavour and all staff would be out of contact until the next day.

They re-crossed the piazza, arm in arm, avoiding acquaintances with a quick wave. Near the fountain, Leah heard Signora Luciapietra say Giulio's name. Leah pulled Nick aside, onto the bench that skirted the fountain.

"What are you..."

"Shhhhh. Listen." She indicated the two women sitting close by.

"...said two hunters found him at the base of the cliff. One was the Antonini man, Leonardo. I heard someone say Giulio had done it for love. Imagine. Him. For love."

Signora Luciapietra's friend leaned closer. "I don't believe it..."

"Believe it or not, it's what I heard. And the Lieutenant's nowhere to be found."

"Well, of course not! If it's true, he's out there dealing with it! And if he isn't, how would I know where he is? A storm is coming; I have to go shopping."

Open mouthed, Signora Luciapietra watched her friend walk away and shouted after her, "Shopping? That's all you can say when someone's just died?"

Chapter Ten

Inside their apartment, Nick clasped Leah in a tight embrace. "Thank god you're safe."

"You're having a delayed reaction, Nick. I'm okay, but if Signora Luciapietra is right, poor Leonardo."

"I'm not having a delayed reaction! I'm angry at you. And I love you all over again. You just can't stop getting into trouble. It drives me crazy. And besides, you're still trembling. You need a shower, some tea, then you can tell me the whole story. We've got to figure out what to do."

"What do you mean, 'What to do'?"

He ignored her question. "If Sergeant Gianicollo is out and Cavour is in the gorge and is going to be out of communication until tomorrow, like the note said, and the only emergency numbers are theirs, there's nothing we can do until tomorrow. I wouldn't tell that tittle-tattle redheaded." He brushed his hand through the air over his head to indicate the secretary's wild red hair.

She's out too, anyway," Leah said.

Nick jerked. "Hair! Thank God you had on that hat and the coat, and you can run like a gazelle. Still, whoever it was that pushed Giulio is going to assume you'll be telling everybody what happened, and everyone in town will know it was you."

He reached for her again, but she held back.

"Enough with the hugs and the worry! You're repeating yourself. I'm okay! You don't have to worry; I feel fine. I'm 100 percent certain he didn't recognize me. And now I'm going to shower and think this through, and

I'm not going to get emotional again. It was the adrenaline and fear of the moment up there." She pointed in the direction of the vie cave. "I'm fine now; it looks like you're the one that's not." She gave him a quick pat on the arm. "How'd you know I was at the dromoi anyway?"

"I didn't, not for sure. But we talked about that spot at the end of that meadow as a good place for a picnic and maybe taking some photos there. Anyway, I thought you might go there..."

He paused. "It probably won't help, but I'll get rid of your hat and jacket. He'll for sure remember the dark blue. I'll leave them in the dumpster near the piazza. The important thing is not to give any clues that it was you."

"He doesn't need clues, Nick! Everybody in town knows I go to the vie cave early mornings. Anyone sitting in the bar would have seen me pass, and the barmaid tells everyone everything. I've just got to get to Cavour. He won't know it was murder. He'll think Giulio fell or committed suicide like Signora Luciapietra said."

"Yes, and you also heard her say that Leonardo and the others found him already. That's where Cavour is. They'll start an investigation, and tomorrow we'll go in, relaxed, casual, and tell Ms. Redhead we need to talk to the Lieutenant about visas. That's what she'll plug into her gossip line. When we get into Cavour's office, we'll give him the disk from the camera, and we can look at the photo close up."

"We could look at it now, on the computer."

"No, we can't."

He looked away.

"I screwed up; I broke the transformer. I didn't want to tell you when we were arguing."

"But..." She put her hand to her mouth and bit her finger.

"Don't bite your finger. I'll get it fixed. You've got your article on a thumb drive, and we can borrow a computer. For now, the important thing is to keep you safe. Anyway, look out the window. It might storm, and reception will be messed up."

"Likely excuse. We could take the photo to Andrea. He could probably enlarge it."

"Leahhh, stop! Think! We can't take it to Andrea. He could print it and enlarge it, you're right, and before long the news would be spread all over town. We can't show it to anyone but Cavour."

Nick wrinkled his forehead. "For now, let's just go on as if things were normal, and get the photo to the Lieutenant as soon as we can."

He fell silent and stared at the floor. "Listen, Francesca will be here soon. You'll be safe with the Antoninis tonight, and I'll see you there when our troupe gets there."

Leah could see Nick's thoughts tumble from one to the next. As frustrated as she sometimes was with his perpetual analyzing, his patient reasoning was one of the things she loved most about him. She thought back over the morning, the excitement of finding the spot for a great photo, the initial disbelief at what she was seeing, the terror of the escape down the trail into the cave, and then the safe haven of Nick. Evil. Good.

Her emotions bolted from one to the next. She tried to read each one: fear, gratitude, anger, terror. Had she been identified? Was it foolish to hope she hadn't? Fear had morphed to anger. Or perhaps they were the same thing. She had been hunted. Did she want revenge? Was she still angry that Nick hadn't come with her?

She wasn't. She was relieved. How was it that in moments of terror and fear of loss, love would arise, fade, then burst, leaving in its wake sometimes a hot, sudden flow of passion, or a cool moment of tenderness like she felt now towards Nick. All this turmoil in tangled threads, all this turmoil wreathed with laughter when strength came.

She was beginning to feel like her old self.

She turned toward the bathroom for her shower, but before she closed the door, she swiveled around and looked back at Nick. "Enough thinking! I need to move, to do something!"

With a jerk of his arm, Nick shook his forefinger at her. "You want to jump into the middle of this and go for the guy. You can't do it, Leah! Tonight's the Befanata and that's what we have to do or my years of work, and yours too, are ruined. You want to be part of a grand adventure, like you've always wanted. But not now. It's too dangerous, and it isn't the right time."

He was right. She wanted to go back to the via cava, to search the table rock for some sort of clue, something that had been dropped, or a boot print in the dust. She wanted to be part of the adventure, even part of the danger.

"I see you! Stop daydreaming and listen to me. The guy is obviously going to be hunting you, but you've got to hold back. It's too dangerous. And we're not leaving a corpse alone in the woods. Leonardo already found Giulio; the Lieutenant already knows, and you'll hear all about it tonight at the Antoninis. We can't give the Lieutenant our information and the photo because they're not back. So just help me today, okay? Be patient and let me do this."

"But the Antoninis are our closest friends and Leonardo found him...."

"And if you tell them now, before we've talked to the Lieutenant, they'll be upset, plus what you know may make things dangerous for them. We don't know anything about the motive for the murder; we don't know how far the tentacles of motive may reach. The safest way is to be quiet for now. Remember that disaster training you took: The greatest good for the greatest number of people."

"Geez...." Leah made a face.

Nick laughed. "Okay. That was a bit much. But it's true. And this way I don't have to miss the Befanata."

"I'll decide what to say when I get to the Antoninis. Would you bring me a towel from downstairs?"

Nick sighed. She would do what she wanted to do.

Chapter Eleven

At midday, before many in town knew of the dead body below the cliff, the owner of the photo shop, Andrea, was bounding across the piazza, his jacket flying out behind him. He had spotted Signora Vianello standing at the door, impatiently shuffling from one foot to the other. He gritted his teeth.

The Signora's fur coat, which she wore except in hottest summer, crouched on her broad shoulders like a bobcat ready to strike. Andrea hated that fur coat, particularly on this day. The coat seemed to be a personal slight to him, a persistent, provocative reminder the Signora was a landowner and he a shopkeeper.

Secondo stood near the fountain, grinning at the sight of Andrea's long legs churning across the piazza. Some called Secondo the town idiot. This was because of his erratic behavior and because he sometimes stood for hours silently watching the townspeople pass back and forth across the piazza. Secondo didn't care what people called him. He liked watching people; and he liked seeing what they would do, particularly when they were upset.

The evening before, two men in the bar had begun to argue. Intent on the scene of the fight—and he saw it as a scene, as if he were a bystander in a movie—Secondo stood in the crowd that had gathered and watched the two men slam each other in the face, on the shoulders, in the stomach. They both had blood on their fists.

People were so strange.

Andrea reached the door of his shop, panting. "I'm here, Signora. Forgive me. I'm sorry you had to wait. I was...I...delayed."

She cringed. He had used the form of address one would use with a good friend, rather than the form one would use with a respected elder. This infraction of manners aggravated her, but she was in a hurry and decided to let it go.

In spite of her frustrations with him, the Signora appreciated Andrea's exceptional talent. This lanky, ill-kempt, but attractive man harbored in the silence of his ostensibly simple life a profound and unique sense of people and places. The Signora always said he could cull beauty from a sty. All this, plus he was one of her good friend, Signora Seta's, nephews, much more talented and amenable than the other nephew, Giulio.

Unfortunate he's never married, the Signora thought as she looked at Andrea. She doubted if now that he was in his late thirties he ever would. Many of his photographs of Scansansianso and the surrounding countryside graced her walls. His style was unique and, being an astute businesswoman, she felt sure he soon would be well-known throughout Italy and beyond.

She sometimes caught a glimpse of him looking at her as if he were angry with her for some slight. At those times, she wondered what she could have done to offend him. *It should be evident I appreciate his artistry*, the Signora thought defensively. He had been in her house many times and had seen that in every room there was at least one of his photos, beautifully framed, cared for. Still, when she spoke with him, she felt uneasy.

Waiting for him, pressured by errands she needed to finish, the Signora became assertive.

"Where have you been? We had an appointment! And what's the matter? Your tie is askew, your feet are muddy…. You look like you've seen a ghost."

He glanced at his feet.

"*Che cavolo!*" he cursed.

"What did you say?"

"There's a broken pipe near my house. I was trying to dam up the little stream of water from it because it runs into my entryway."

Infuriated with himself for such a stupid excuse and with her for being nosy, Andrea struggled to control himself. He could not afford to respond. She knew he was lying, and he knew she knew it.

"It looks like you've been in the woods! All that mud. I've been waiting twenty minutes! I need the photos now! I promised to have them for my friends' anniversary celebration, so catch your breath and get this done!"

Andrea's face turned bright red, and sweat from the exertion of the run poured from under his long hair down the sides of his face. Feeling beaten by the club of her words, he regarded her without speaking. She wore a heavy coat of face powder, dark, clumped mascara, and bright red lipstick. In an attempt to make her cheekbones appear higher—they were high as it was—she had spotted them with rouge, which she'd forgotten to blend into her makeup. Below the rouge, her jowls sagged with the weight of her seventy years.

Andrea gritted his teeth, stepped forward, and fumbled with the key.

"Wait here, I'll get the switch."

Inside, he stepped carefully around the stand of tourist postcards he had created for the summer visitors and felt his way along the edge of his desk until he reached the light switch on the far wall. Illuminated, the bare bulb in the ceiling cast a dim glow over the little room. Except for the desk and a small printer set on a stand, the room was empty, but the walls were covered with historic photos of Scansansiano in the late 1800s. There was a photo of two peasant men sitting at the fountain in the middle of the piazza; one of a woman in her long, dark skirt hanging out laundry; a group of boys frozen in mid-kick as they played soccer in the piazzetta. Intermingled with the historical photos were contemporary shots Andrea had taken himself: A bird's eye view of the river below town, an artistic shot of a newly plowed field at the edge of the forest. Below the walls, stacks two to three feet deep of framed photos and photos printed on aluminum leaned against every wall.

"Why don't you clean this place, Andrea? You have so many beautiful pieces. If you owned land, you would care for it a little better, no? This is your property."

Andrea clenched his jaw.

"Well..." the Signora prodded him.

"There's a method in my madness, Signora. I take care of my photos—and yours—very well." He glared at her. She could not conceive of the strain he was under.

Startled by his response, the Signora stepped back.

Andrea, unable to control himself after the morning's events, snarled, "As they say, 'Neatness in moderation is a virtue, but carried to extremes narrows the mind.'"

The Signora burst out, her face an angry red. "Don't address me in the familiar!"

His mood suddenly calm, Andrea glanced out the window, then turned to her, a stiff smile on his face. "Never mind, Signora. I apologize doubly. And you're right. I should take better care." He spread his open palms in a wide half-circle. "It is as it is. It may look like a mess, but I do know each photo, and I know where each is. Not neat enough for your tastes, but organized enough for mine."

"Well, it looks like chaos to me." She gave a self-righteous shake of her head.

He picked up an envelope from his desk and held it toward her, daring her to step toward him and take it. "Your photos, at my fingertips, you see? I'm sorry I was late."

She took a quick step forward, snatched the envelope, and retreated to the doorway. "Thank you. I'll pay you tomorrow. I'm late for...."

Her words were carried away by the wind. She rushed off, leaving the door open behind her.

"Tomorrow then," Andrea said to her back. He drew a deep breath, slumped into his chair, and wiped the sweat from his face with his shirt sleeve. "I've got other things to think about."

Chapter Twelve

Signora Vianello walked toward her car wondering why her interchange with Andrea had been antagonistic. *He was a fine artist, and they both knew she appreciated his work. Why had he been agitated? Why had she been abrupt? It was unlike her. What was wrong with him?*

Passing the bar facing the piazza, she noticed Angelina rush up the steps and flop down in a chair next to the window across from her friend, Giovanna. The Signora stopped to watch them as they leaned toward each other in a rapid, intense conversation, their arms slicing the air with gestures. Repelled by their haphazard dress and their often-times impertinent behavior, she shook her head.

How anyone will ever buy real estate from either of those two is beyond me. Angelina has not even an iota of manners, and Giovanna is a mean, spiteful girl. Sad. She was so sweet before she got involved with those men. They're wasting their money taking courses in real estate.

Raised in an earlier generation as a Venetian lady, the Signora came from a background of comfort and delicacy, if not true wealth. She had attended Liceo Marco Foscarini, the oldest high school in Venice and had studied music at the *Conservatorio di Musica Benedetto Marcello di Venezia*. She and her parents had enjoyed Venetian holidays like the Redentore, when they decorated their boat with garlands and flags, tucked a basket of food and wine in the bow, and wafted slowly along the canals to the *bacino*, the broad expanse of water between the San Marco neighborhood and the island of San Giorgio. From the bacino, they watched the fireworks and ate, their garlands fluttering above them in the breeze.

Schooled in this way to dress and behave in the formal Venetian manner, the Signora's sense of decorum had been roughed at the edges since she had moved to the small village of Scansansiano, but not enough to erase her repugnance for scruffy dress and unclean habits. The Signora had suffered years of poverty and loss, the story of which few Scansansiand knew, but those that did know her history knew she had lived her hard years with dignity and pride. Her frustration was for those who could do better but chose not to, not for those who had no means to do better.

Most people are unaware of the true lives of the people they meet, just as the Signora was ignorant of the full histories of Angelina and Giovanna. Andrea too had his ideas as he sat in his studio watching the Signora watch the two young women, and thinking of all that had happened in just hours.

Chapter Thirteen

Inside the bar, Giovanna and Angelina saw the Signora stand, stare, and pass on.

"Look at her!" Giovanna quipped. "That coat! Will she ever get rid of it? It looks like dog fur."

"Forget about her!" Angelina hissed. Ignoring her own piercings, she taunted, "And look at yourself. Nose rings, earrings, lip studs, eyebrow studs... There's so much silver crap all over your face I can't figure out where Silvio finds room to kiss you....Or does he kiss you...?" Her face twisted in a lewd grin.

Giovanna ignored her. "She's the biggest landowner around."

"Who cares? Signora Seta's cantina is probably the equal or more to all Vianello's property."

"What do you suppose she ever came here for?" Giovanna mused.

The Signora was a perennial source of mystery. Why she had moved so far from her beloved Venice, her native dialect, her society of fur coats and gold, few knew. Like Giovanna and Angelina, many wondered about her, teased her behind her back and sometimes to her face, yet offered her a begrudging respect. The Signora received this tainted attention with equanimity and grace. The mystery of why she had moved so far from the lagoon, so far from a life on water, few knew.

Angelina jabbed Giovanna's arm. "Let's just concentrate on Signora Seta. She's the important one."

"Her cantina is worth that much? Giulio said..."

"Giulio is a no-good lowlife, even if he is Seta's nephew, Angelina blurted out.

"I know! He's a jerk." Giovanna spat it out, tapping hard with her middle finger on the table. "Someday he'll get what he deserves. But why'er you calling him a no-good. I thought..."

Angelina looked away. "I think Italo trusts him too much. He's not only a dealer; he's high as a kite a lot of the time." She paused to stare at her friend before continuing, "So you think he'll get what he deserves, huh? I didn't realize *you* hated him so much. I thought you two were an item."

"The bastard uses people. He's no better than my dad – or yours." She turned aside and spat on the floor.

"Hey!" The barmaid yelled. "This isn't a barn. Get outa here if you're gonna act like that."

Giovanna held up her palms. "I didn't really spit anything; it was just air."

"Air or not. It's disgusting. This is a decent place."

"Okay, okay."

Angelina grabbed Giovanna's arm. "Forget about Giulio. You don't need him. Italo will get the cantina, and then you'll come to work with us." She picked up the ashtray and held it in both hands, turning it round and round. "And you can go to Rome for what you need."

Giovanna jerked away, rubbing her arm where Angelina's grasp had abraded her skin. She stared at her friend, uncertain whether to be angry or to laugh it off. They had always talked, but not about everything. *How in the hell did Angelina know about the drugs?* Her laugh came out high, pinched. "So you know a few things. Okay. But how do you know Italo will get the cantina?"

"Well, I hope he does."

The two women had been friends since confirmation classes with Don Alonso. A pale, thin, long-legged, and nervous thirteen-year-old, Angelina had joined the class a year before confirmation, when her father forced her to go.

"Because of your own guilt!" she yelled, "because you're hoping God will forgive you through me! But He won't!"

Sitting next to each other during lessons, the girls recognized the bruises, the bite marks on each other's arms and necks. In the painful camaraderie of abuse, they became instant friends who told each other many of the details of their lives, if not the worst.

Angelina changed the subject. "We could have a real-life here, Italo and I, and you working with us."

She dropped the ashtray.

Startled, Giovanna blurted, "Right, right! Let's forget the old stuff. Water under the bridge. Each house has its own passions, right?"

The barmaid was glaring at them. They sipped their coffee. Intensified by the glass of the long window, the sun warmed them, and they sat in a nervous silence, their hands moving continually, tapping the table, turning the ashtray.

Giovanna broke the silence. "What's up with you anyway? You look like you haven't slept in 3 or 4 nights—and haven't showered either."

Angelina snapped, "You don't look so good yourself! Your shoes are covered with mud and you're sweaty, even though it's cold." She thrust a thumb over her shoulder, "And if she notices your feet, you'll get kicked out of here."

Giovanna glanced down at her shoes. "Damn it!"

"Come on. I was joking; they're not that bad."

"I was…I was on the steps down below town. I dropped something there yesterday and didn't have time to clean up."

"Yeah, right." Angelina grinned. "You were doin' a deal, weren't you?" She leaned closer.

"I wasn't!"

"Shttttt!" Angelina looked to see if anyone had heard. "It's okay. I don't give a damn one way or the other."

Giovanna changed the subject. "How come you're not working?"

"I gave myself the day off to study. So what?"

"So nothing. I don't care. But really? Study? Good for you. I should study." Giovanna popped the knuckles of both hands.

Giovanna and Angelina's conversations were full of minor evasions and petty lies. No matter how similar their histories, they kept secrets, a habit learned from the threats showered on them by their fathers. Even knowing what they knew about each other, their conversations, their banter was a dance with a loaded gun. Secrets confided could be dangerous, could bring down a shower of brutal and inescapable consequences.

Each of these two women lived a paradox. Both were publicly known victims of abuse, yet each carried an ocean of secrets below the public knowledge.

Now, in front of her friend, at the suggestion of impossible dreams in which the three of them worked together in happy unison, Giovanna struggled to resist the urge to confide and release the burden of one of these subterranean creatures by diverting it to foolishness.

Her words tumbled out by their own volition, irrelevant. Tight-lipped, she spoke in the rough Italian she had learned at home. "I wish I had a dog. But the only place I could walk it without a leash would be the vie cave, and I never go there, never!"

She had barely averted a confession.

"Geez, what's the matter with you? I get it! You never go there!"

"The trails are too damned eerie." She rambled on, "I mean even during the day, and anyway, living in town, I couldn't have a dog."

"What's with the dog thing all of a sudden? If you want a dog, let me sell you an apartment further out." She grinned. Giovanna couldn't buy an apartment if her life depended on it, and she couldn't sell Giovanna one without a license.

"I know I can't have a dog, let alone an apartment. I'm just talking." Her expansive hoop earrings wobbled against her neck. "How's Italo?"

Angelina gave a slow, sinuous smile, and shook her head. "You're completely wacko today! He's fine, why?"

"Nothing. I just wondered. He reminds me of your father."

"Dumbass! That's how much you know! Italo's never beat me... and never done anything else either. And he never will."

"C'mon Angelina. We all say that, but the conversation's always the same: 'He promised he would never do it again, but the next day I....' and then you fill in how it was all your fault because you provoked him."

41

"Shut up. You don't know anything about Italo. He's a lot of talk, but a real fluff at heart."

"Sure, and when I saw him kick a dog almost to death when it crossed him one day, that was just fluff."

"A dog's different."

"Not for us it isn't."

"You're an idiot. He's good to me." There were tears in her eyes.

"Good God, Angelina, whaterya cryin for? It's embarrassing. You said he's good to you."

"It's not that. It's just…things. There are things I wish I could erase." She grasped Giovanna by the arm.

Giovanna pulled roughly away and charged into a hissed tirade, furious with Angelina because of her own pain. "Don't get started again. I can see it in your eyes, damn you. Your dad is your dad. He's a bastard, and he always will be. If you don't like it, move out. He'll never stop. We've been over this a hundred times. I want to forget about what happened to me, and I sure as hell don't want more of the same crap on my shoulders from you. Our fathers make me want to kill somebody. What happened to me was not my fault. And it wasn't yours when you were a kid, but now it is, damn it because you stick around. Good God! Just get out!" She shouted the last words.

The room went silent.

Giovanna's face turned red. She lowered her voice and whispered. "Just let it go. You've got Italo; he doesn't lie to you, doesn't ever really beat you, doesn't force himself on you—and that's a hell of a lot more than a lot of us have had."

Angelina sat up straight in her chair and wiped her eyes. She stared at Giovanna, cleared her throat, and sniffed. "You're right. What's done is done." She looked down at the floor. "I can't change what happened. I didn't do it because I wanted to. And, I do have Italo. I like being a mistress; no sniveling little kids around, fine meals, good wine, a vacation now and then, and somebody who has no say over me."

"See. I'm telling you, we've got it good." Giovanna didn't mention again that Angelina was still living with her father.

42

Angelina nodded,"I went to school with Italo's wife, did you know that? She knows about me and Italo, but she stays down on the coast. I stay here, and we don't bother each other. I couldn't stand it if Italo started up with some other woman. I don't know how she does." She turned the ashtray round and round in her hands. "Italo will get the cantina, we'll have a restaurant, and it will be a real life."

"Don't be so certain about the cantina. It's good Giulio's oldest. If Signora Seta sticks to tradition, she will give the cantina to him." She emitted a rude guffaw. "Unless Giulio is back in the doghouse. From the scuttlebutt, it seems like Seta wavers on the cantina every other day."

"It'll work out." Angelina set the ashtray carefully in the center of the table and twirled it again.

"Think so?"

"Andrea's the nicer. He'll be the one to inherit, and all he wants are Signora Seta's old photos. Once he gets those, he'll sell the cantina to Italo, and then Italo and I…"

"Dream on, sweetie. You're right about Andrea, but like I said, Seta is a wildcard, you can never tell what she will do, so who knows what'll happen? And maybe she'll split the inheritance? Maybe give the photos to Andrea and the cantina to Giulio or someone else? And besides, I thought Andrea didn't like Italo."

They fell silent and stared through the window at the scud clouds flowing overhead.

Chapter Fourteen

The Signora drove away deep in thought. From her first arrival in town, there were some citizens who had received her soft-spoken, discreet help in one way or another. Those who didn't know her, who were ignorant of the significance of her fur coat, or who denigrated her character, were those who had yet had no inkling of her hidden generosity. And even to some who knew, the joking about her coat was simply the gentle teasing of one loved and respected.

As she drove along, the Signora herself was wondering what help she could possibly give to Angelina and Giovanna. Perhaps, the help to escape. Angelina was the daughter of a man who, in his youth had left town, eager for America. Certain he would become rich overnight, he borrowed from his brothers, made his way to Genoa, and sailed for the U.S.

Life in America was not like the stories he had heard from the town gossip. His lack of friends and support, plus his poor knowledge of English, defeated him in the end, and he came home disillusioned, angry, tail between his legs, ready to carry his frustration and defeat into marriage with a former classmate. The children came each year, small, powerless, easy marks for anger, and for the girls, sexual abuse.

About Giovanna, the Signora knew little, except that she was studying for her real estate license. Like Angelina, mistress of the buffoon Italo, Giovanna was the lover of another out-of-towner, Silvio.

Studying for a real estate license! The both of them! Ridiculous! They need to be realistic, to take a good look at themselves.

All the Signora could hope was that Angelina and Giovanna would find a way to escape the men who made the deep bruises on their arms.

These young women, and others, taunted the Signora about her coat, but she accepted it. Few people knew that her inclination to wear her fur coat even on weekdays was not arrogance, but a habit that had filtered down from her Venetian ancestors, ancestors accustomed to wealth and show. The coat had been her mother's, and before that, her grandmother's, carefully refurbished by the furrier and mended by the tailor down the street. In even the poorest times, the hardest years, she had saved the coat, and when she climbed from the pit of her poverty, she wore it with pride as a mark of her history, as a mark of her perseverance through tragedy. Wearing the coat, she made the *passegiata,* the evening stroll through the piazza, with her head high, little caring what the others thought. She acknowledged that part of her longed for the days of decorum when people wore fur coats, and with the exception of the closest friends, addressed each other in the formal manner, aware of the beauty of decorum. She acknowledged this in herself, but only in passing. She had become a woman of courage, a woman capable of facing reality.

These thoughts on her mind, she hurried on, her honest, charitable heart obscured by the thick fur.

Chapter Fifteen

Late afternoon, there was a knock on the door at Nick and Leah's. Nick opened it to Francesca Antonini, the teenage daughter of their friends, Leonardo Antonini, and his wife, Anna Pellini. Francesca's long dark hair twisted in the late afternoon breeze and her dark eyes reflected a deep sadness.

"Come in, Francesca; I hope you didn't get caught in the storm." Nick stood back, motioning toward the small, flowered couch that faced the kitchen side of the room.

"No, it passed so quickly it almost wasn't there."

"How's your dad?"

"He's distraught. Something like this, it never happened before."

"Signora Benvenuto said he was the one who found Giulio. How did it happen?"

Nick glanced at Leah.

"We don't know. Giulio knows the trails, and it doesn't make sense he was on the table rock. Dad was off work today and out hunting. He was headed downriver to meet his friend near the bridge, and he said he heard a scream. When he looked up he saw a man grasping at the air and then fall through the trees."

Tears pooled in her eyes. "He'll tell you about it when you get there."

Nick hugged her. "I'm sorry. I didn't mean to make you cry."

"We've never had anything like this happen before, and dad says they think it might be murder."

"Why?" Leah blurted.

Francesca's head jerked, surprised at Leah's sharp voice. "I don't know. Dad will tell you. He was the one who called Lieutenant Cavour, and he stayed with Giulio until the Lieutenant came. A good thing he caught the Lieutenant in time. Service is out again."

"Everything seems scombobulated." Leah made a face.

With the tears still glistening on her cheeks, Francesca burst into laughter at Leah's characteristic attempt to combine an English and an Italian word. "*Scombussolato*," she corrected, with a tug at Leah's arm. "We'd better go. There are more cakes to make."

Leah and Francesca walked through the fading light along the narrow street, which rose in a gentle incline toward the piazza and the parking lot on the far side, the last point cars were allowed into the historic center. Their backs were to the west, and the last light of day curved eastward, around their dark forms. They moved slowly, both women silent. Leah carried the burden of her secret, and the teenage Francesca struggled to absorb the reality that someone she knew had died a violent death.

A wind rose and now rushed through the corridor of the narrow street. As if choreographed, both women pulled their coats close around their necks to block the chill of the wind's fingers at their throats. In the deepening gloom, they kept silent, stepping in unison, their footsteps echoing along the walls.

At the tiny *piazzetta* in front of the church, pigeons swooped overhead in one graceful motion, like the stroke of a pen marking a broad, black letter in the sky. Leaning into the hill, the two women came to the edge of the main piazza. There, in front of the bakery, just next to the bar, Andrea, Silvio, and Giovanna were huddled in a compact circle, smoke from their cigarettes twirling wildly in the wind.

Leah barely knew the three of them. Silvio owned a tourist shop with Giulio; Andrea had the photo shop. Leah had heard that Giovanna, Silvio's girlfriend, was studying for her real estate license, but otherwise, she seemed unemployed. Leah had seen her wandering through town, sometimes in the morning, sometimes in the afternoon.

In the way of the town, Leah and Francesca stopped to greet the three. It was a desultory encounter with slight nods, somber faces, and the mandatory handshakes. Leah regarded dark-eyed Giovanna. Her face was studded with heavy, metal piercings through her eyebrows, nose, ears, and even tongue. She stood close beside Silvio, who was equally metaled, and had cut his hair in Mohawk fashion.

The lanky, sloe-eyed Andrea stood to the side, the small but sullen distance a hint to his solitary character, a signal that he preferred to guard his privacy.

The ritual of shaking hands befuddled Leah. From childhood, her father had taught her that a handshake should be firm, yet in Scansansiano it was more of a brushing of the palms. Leah found the quick slide of palm against palm to be disconcerting, given her own hardy character. She could not read the visceral spirit in such a light touch of hands.

It was the two-cheek kiss that made her feel most at home: the coming together in an almost embrace, the delicate graze of skin on skin, the fresh smell of soap. This ritual with close friends established an immediate warmth and amity, but there was no connection with these three that allowed or urged such a kiss.

Silvio was the first to speak, but his words flew upward with the wind, and Leah missed what he was saying. When he raised his voice, she heard, "…a sad Befanata."

Sorting through the thick silver nose rings, a lip ring, and the two silver bubbles joined by a shaft through the outer edge of his eyebrows, Leah noted he was a handsome, small-boned man, of average height, with a high forehead, aquiline nose, and hands that gestured gracefully as he spoke. She could not envision him in the army, he seemed so slight, but she knew from the Signora he had been in service and had served with distinction. Now he stood in front of her, eyes glassy from drugs, his arms hanging loosely at his sides, leaning a little, as if resting his shoulder against an invisible wall.

Giovanna inclined toward him. Her long, lusterless hair twisted over her cheek and wisped upward in the wind. She brushed the hair away from her face with short, blunt fingers and pulled at the threads of hair caught on her nose stud. Carefully unwinding the hair, she tucked it back over her ear, revealing large silver-hoop earrings, twins of Silvio's. Unlike her limpid hair, her eyelashes were exceptionally long and thick, and Leah felt a pang of jealously.

Giovanna's drug habit was new enough that even glassy-eyed, she was lovely of face if one disregarded the metal, and Leah noted the sensual pull her full figure had on both Silvio and Andrea.

Andrea was the enigma. Average, he was handsome in the way a person full of life is handsome. Not counting what appeared to Leah to be his unreciprocated attraction to Giovanna, Leah knew he had two loves: music and old photos. When he sang—Leah had heard him with a group near the fountain one night—or when he spoke about his photos, it was as if his face gathered all the ambient light, and he exuded an infectious excitement to those around him. His nose was slightly askew on his face, and his ears too large for his head, but when he held his guitar, he brightened and became as handsome as any man Leah had seen. She once watched him in the large reception room of the city offices, playing for a town festival. Giving himself totally to the music, his eyes glistened and danced like candlelight, and the people in the audience gathered close around, enthralled by his passion for the music, all yearning to capture his intensity, as if to suckle and nurture their own spirits.

This early evening, all three friends appeared subdued, windblown, wrapped like phantoms in wild shrouds of smoke. Still, Leah had lived in Scansansiano for months each year, enough to know all three of them were flesh and blood and could become furiously angry.

Now, in the dim light of the bakery windows, she studied their faces, wondering if, in anger, one of them could have shoved Giulio off the cliff, or if they were all simply prone to the normal, protean emotions, less guarded than most.

"Hmmh," Andrea grunted, looking from side to side and over his shoulder, as if to see if anyone were watching.

"What'er ya looking for, yesterday?" Giovanna poked Andrea in the ribs.

Andrea struck out with a backhand, which Giovanna evaded only by a quick dodge to the right.

"Good God, Andrea, what's the matter with you? I was only joking." She stepped further away.

Andrea stared at her, his face flushed with anger. "Don't fool with me. I'm not in the mood."

"You're never in the mood. All you think about are those lousy photos—and you won't even get them."

"What do you know? They're as good as mine, right now."

"Well, maybe Signora Seta will have something to say about that; even with Giulio gone, she may decide to give them to someone else, or at least the cantina. And if you don't get both, you won't have any money to do anything with the photos anyway."

She stepped forward, flicked her finger under his chin, and jumped back, huddling against Silvio, who was grinning.

"Shut up! Just shut up." Andrea yelled.

Anticipating a fight, Leah felt her muscles tense. She stepped forward to stop the fight before it started, but Andrea stood still, his head bent, his arms at his sides.

Seeing she was in no danger from Andrea, Giovanna spoke, "Some people have been saying we should cancel the Befanata, but we're going ahead with it. Giulio would want us to. He loved the Befanata, and if nothing else we should do it for him."

Silvio bristled, "Yeah, and you would know what Giulio wanted, wouldn't you!"

Giovanna tossed her head and glared defiantly, making her hair twist wildly in the wind, "Yes, as a matter of fact, I would."

Silvio threw his cigarette butt to the street and ground it viciously back and forth as if it were an insect.

As Leah watched, she recognized in them a tinge of the tempestuous relationships of her parents. Theirs had been more genteel perhaps, but still stormy, unsettling, and she had seen what a waste of passion and life those emotions were when enacted. When the anger and impatience of her parents leaked into her own heart, Leah struggled to contain herself. Watching Silvio and Giovanna, she was thankful her daughter Sara and Jonathan were of gentle, patient character. She wanted to reach out to these three young people in front of her, to tell them what a waste of time and life impulsive passions could be.

Andrea put his hands palm to palm and shook them up and down. "My God, Giulio's dead. He's dead. Let it go between the two of you, at least for tonight. Let it be the Befanata."

Silvio turned on him like a snake, hissing. "Oh, right! Just like you let it go? Even if you don't, you should. You're closer to the photo collection than ever now, right? And where were you this morning?"

Giovanna piped up, "Yeah? And back with mud all over your boots?"

Andrea turned and stalked away.

Francesca, who had stood in a stunned silence, pulled at Leah's coat sleeve, drawing her away with a little wave to the group, "See you later."

Across the piazza, Leah leaned toward Francesca, "What was that all about?"

"Oh, I don't know. There's so much gossip. Let's talk about something else—like Sara's wedding. I don't want to think about these sad things anymore."

"Well, about Sara's wedding…"

Chapter Sixteen

Silvio and Giovanna watched the two women walk away.

"Two goody-goodies, and the angry photographer," Silvio snarled.

"Andrea is touchy. Did 'ya see how he slapped at my hand?"

"He had a tiff with fur coat today."

"Everybody has tiffs with her once in a while. That's nothing new."

"Then figure it out for yourself!"

"Wow! You too? What's wrong? And why didn't you show up at our place today?" Giovanna tugged at Silvio's coat.

A cloud of guilt passed over Silvio's face. "I had something else to do."

"Like what?" Giovanna stuck out her chin.

"It's none of your damn business. Lay off."

Giovanna stood stock still, her face reddening in anger. With exaggerated motions, she lit a cigarette and bent to brush away a tattered wrapper the wind had blown against her leg. As she leaned forward, a necklace slipped out of her blouse.

"What's that?"

Silvio reached for the necklace.

Giovanna jumped back.

"Just a bauble."

"It's not a bauble!" He grabbed the necklace, his face contorted in an ugly mask of jealousy. "It's Giulio's bullet. He's had it since we were in the army together."

"So?"

"So what the hell are you doing with it? It's his good luck charm, but he didn't have it…"

"He gave it to me."

"I knew it. God damn it, I knew it… When did he give it to you?"

"What difference does it make? It's just an old bullet."

Silvio jerked the chain from around her neck. Giovanna toppled forward against him. With a swift snap of his arms he pushed her off.

"I knew it! He stole my half of the drug money, and he screwed around with you. And you, you goddamned whore. I was right! I'm glad I gave him what he deserved!"

"What do you mean, you gave him what he deserved? Silvio, you didn't…?" Her eyes glistened with the terror of what she understood.

Silvio shoved by her. "Shut your mouth, bitch!" He glanced around to see if anyone were near. "Would I have?"

The barber from the shop across the street stepped out of his doorway and was staring at them. Seeing him, Silvio hurried away toward the *piazzetta* below.

"Stinking lowlife!" Giovanna yelled after him, "I could…"

Silvio spun around. "You could what? Kill me? Try. Giulio's gone, but I'm still here, so try whatever you want, bitch."

He turned and stomped away, punching the air with his fist. Dangling through his fingers, the chain and the bullet hoicked back and forth, as if it wanted to escape.

When Silvio was out of sight, Giovanna dug in her pocket for a tissue, lifted the hair from her neck, and swiped at the bleeding cut the chain had made. Anger whipped through her veins like a cloth in a strong wind, and her face contorted with fury.

The barber stepped toward her. "If I were you," he said, jabbing his finger at her, "I'd watch what I say these days."

She made the rude gesture of the umbrella and strode down the darkened alley that led to her apartment. She would make up with Silvio. He would never relinquish his obsession for her, but she could not scrub her thoughts of what had happened when she met Giulio below town the day before his death.

They had been standing at the bottom of the wooden steps that led to a lower via cava, ready to make the usual exchange of money for meth. For no reason she could understand, he told her he was cutting her off. When she protested, he tried to soothe her. She was infuriated.

"Come on, Giovanna, it's for your own good. It's supposed to be fun, sweetie, but you're getting out of hand. And…I need my bullet back."

"It's supposed to be fun, sweetie," she mimicked. "I need my bullet back, sweetie; it's my little good luck charm, sweetie." She spat the words. "Listen, shithead, you're the one who got me hooked, remember? And I pay you. You're the one…oh, never mind, but you'd better watch your back! One of these days someone who depends on you won't put up with it anymore."

She shoved him hard against the wooden railing, which was rotted and weak from years of rain and humidity. Giulio staggered backward and tumbled into the thick brush of the hillside.

Giovanna turned and ran up the steep steps toward town. Midway she stopped to yell back at him.

He called for her to come back, but she swiveled around and pounded upward, surprisingly strong and agile. Around a hairpin curve, she was startled to meet Secondo. He opened his mouth to speak, but before he could Giovanna pushed past him and bolted upward toward the main street. In the piazza she rushed to the bar, searching for the greasy-haired Ottavio, who sometimes had drugs.

After, Giovanna played the scene over and over in her head, struggling with the torment of one who has something to hide. Had Secondo heard when she yelled at Giulio that she hoped someone would butcher him? Would Secondo tell? Had anyone seen her at Giulio's door in the dark, early morning of his death, tapping on his door, cursing the silence within as she shuddered against the chill and her desperate need?

Chapter Seventeen

At the same time, Francesca and Leah were on the way to the Antoninis, Signora Seta, native Scansansianese, regular churchgoer, and owner of the finest cantina in town, was packing for a visit to her friend on the coast. Just as she placed the last blouse carefully on top of her other clothes and snapped the suitcase shut, she was startled by a loud pounding on the outside door. Police pounded like that, asserting their terrible authority, too often bearers of bad news.

Signora Seta clasped her robe tightly around her and shuffled to the door, heart pounding with the certainty there had been some horrible accident. Andrea, Giulio, or one of her friends was dead. Her mind always traveled the worst road, and she opened the door carefully as if by being careful she could ward off the inevitable.

The person in front of her seemed familiar, but she could not remember the name. And she didn't understand why this strange person stepped into the entryway and forced her down the stairs into the apartment.

It happened fast. Her weak attempt to fight back. The knife in the stomach. The wrenching pain. The shove into the hole. The blow of landing. The blood. The blood! And the sudden realization that these moments, sucking stale air and smuts of rock refuse, were to be her last moments on earth.

Lying on the cold stone at the bottom of the hole, not quite dead, she felt less fear than befuddlement. Why would someone she didn't know do this? How long would it take to die? Or could she hope, beyond hope, someone might come to save her?

How cold she felt. *Loss of blood*, she reasoned in an oddly lackadaisical way.

She thought of her nephews. It had been wrong of her to waffle on her decision and then surprise them at that meeting. If someone saved her, she would make it right. *But other than my indecision,* she rationalized, *I've been a simple but fairly good person. Neighborly, weekly flowers for the church, gifts when they were needed for my nephews... Why this?*

There was no answer to her question, the last question she would ever ask on earth. It didn't matter. Now, at the end, the Signora was thinking of a line in a poem from the American poet, Emily Dickinson: "Dying is a wild night and a new road."

She had experienced the 'wild night' and now, she thought, 'the new road,' another adventure.

Thus, her death, the death of a believer, drifted over her with unusual calm and only a smidgeon of embarrassment for the poor people who would discover her violated, broken body and would have the duty to take her up, clean the mess, and bury her.

Chapter Eighteen

Francesca guided the little green Fiat around the last curve and turned into the sloping driveway. Tito, the family sheepdog, lurched forward and bounded to the length of his chain barking wildly, straining against the confines of the strong metal links.

Francesca pulled the car forward, at an angle away from Tito, until the bumper almost touched the house. "It's always the same; I'm sorry, Leah. He'll never stop being a guard dog."

Leah smiled. She knew to give Tito a wide berth. He was of the old stock, of the Maremmana Abruzzese breed, chillingly white, black nose, tail set low, and an aloof personality. His deep, rounded ribcage extended below his elbows, and he exuded a sense of prodigious power. Waist tall to Leah, the dog was Leonardo's, a one man, one family dog, bred for the flocks, where he moved among the sheep as one of their own. The flocks were gone, but Tito's breeding persisted, and only Leonardo's voice could stop the dog's onslaught once he sensed a threat to his master or family.

Leah treated the dog's dislike of outsiders with good spirit. Still, each time she came to the farmhouse and heard Tito's barking rip the air and saw him straining against his chain, muscles visibly taut under fur, a shiver ran up her spine.

The gravel crunched underfoot as they walked around the side of the house to the kitchen door. Across the drive in the garden, the dusty-green leaves of the olive trees flickered in the gentle breeze and waning light. Below the trees, next to the walkway, the spiked spines of last year's artichoke plants spread in a ragged circle, one against the other. Leah thought of summer, of the pasta Francesca's mother, Anna, served with fresh squash blossoms. She remembered the tomato sauce and bean soups she had eaten at the Antonini's long dining-room table, accompanied by wine from their grapes. She paused with her hand on the doorknob and gazed out, over the barn and shed, over the valley where the Leora River threaded its way to the sea, and above to the hills, turned shadows by the dim light of the late winter afternoon. It was, it should be, idyllic, she thought.

Francesca waited behind Leah. A mature seventeen, she understood what Leah was seeing, and she too was thinking it should be idyllic, as it always had been for her. Unusual among her peers, she loved life on their small farm, with her parents, grandparents, and brothers when they were home, all working together, while her father ran an accountant's office in the city. The weekends they were all home were joyous reunions when family and friends sat together for hours over a meal made from the fruits of the farm.

Now, a murder, like a worm in the apple of the community. Giulio had been one of her father's classmates at school. Younger than Leonardo, and not a close friend, still they had all known him, and Francesca had hoped to learn accordion from him so she could participate in the Befanata.

Inside, Francesca's mother, Anna, and Anna's mother, Rosetta, were scuttling about the kitchen, while Francesca's paternal grandmother, Carla, stood to the side. Carla's apron was dusted with flour, and having just rinsed her hands after kneading dough, she was drying them in slow careful movements with a yellow hand towel.

A heavy iron woodstove, sat tight against its gas counterpart, pouring heat into the room.

Anna bent to retrieve a pizza from the oven and set it on the marble worktable. Finished, she embraced Leah with the sides of her arms, keeping her flour-dusted hands at a distance. They kissed each other delicately on both cheeks.

"Leah."

She spoke the name softly, with gentle affection, and backed away, arms open. "I'm hot and sweaty."

Sprinkles of flour mottled her clothes and her cheeks shone bright red.

Leah smiled. "Hot and sweaty doesn't bother me." She gave Anna a real hug, and they both laughed; only a slight mist in their eyes betrayed the profound sadness of the day.

Intimidated by these women on first meeting them, because of her mediocre language skills, with time Leah had come to feel at ease and to love them. All of them possessed the qualities of womanhood Leah most admired, and she felt fortunate to be in their company. They were women who knew how to turn pain into power, to find happiness on their own. They worked hard, cared profoundly about family and friends, were generous to the bone, brought intensity and the desire for perfection to every task, and yielded their opinions on a range from politics to childcare with elegant probity and confidence in their own understanding. These were women whose spirits she wanted to carry with her, to instruct her.

"So many pizzas! They're beautiful! I'm surprised Piero and Donato haven't eaten at least half of them!" Leah exclaimed, opening her palms toward the dozen square pizzas on the counter.

Anna answered, "Friends from university invited them for tonight, so they didn't come home. In a way I'm glad…. Take a piece of the pizzetti I've cut. They're plain, but it's what people like most. Dough and tomato sauce, and of course a few white ones as well." She turned to scoot more into the oven.

Francesca piped up, "Wait! Don't eat until you see the desserts in the other room. Mamma made them all." She beamed with pride at her mother.

Leah and Anna were the same height, just over five feet, and nearly the same build. Unlike Leah's long curls, Anna had straight, glistening brown hair pulled back from her face. Her cheeks glowed from the heat in the kitchen and from the wind and sun of the olive grove and garden. Her hands showed the veins and strength of a woman accustomed to hard work. Leah knew that when Anna hugged her, she meant it.

She also knew that Anna would never hug her or invite her if she weren't welcome. Joyous in company and in work, she was a woman impatient with foolishness, quick to perceive falsehood, and willing to speak her keen mind on any subject from friendship to politics. But the most captivating part of her character was her laughter and her insistent urging for Leonardo to tell another of his jokes, especially jokes about the national police.

Leah remembered the police jokes. Now, looking at the woman in front of her, she recalled one from the last time she had eaten with the Antoninis. The room had filled with uproarious laughter. Leonardo was a gifted storyteller. In time, they would laugh again at his jokes, but for now, the laughter was gone.

Anna's grace reminded Leah of her own midwestern farm upbringing and the strength of the women she had grown up among. Like them, Anna was inured to hard work and, like the other farm women, was accustomed to taking over while her husband was away. On the Antonini's small land holding, Anna, with the help of her mother, Rosetta, and Francesca, pruned olive trees, helped butcher, and on the same day, served a dinner of thick, homemade bean soup, roast lamb, oven potatoes with rosemary, green salad, and torte. *Hard work spotlights the character of people*, Leah remembered reading. It was true of Anna, whose every act was built on values of honesty, love of life, and work.

Rosetta stood in her characteristic stance, arms crossed with elbows cupped in her palms. She had been watching the interchange between her daughter and Leah, waiting until she deemed it appropriate to step forward and hug Leah with her own embrace. After she had kissed Leah on both cheeks, Rosetta grasped her shoulders and looked straight into her eyes.

"Leah."

She spoke only the one word, but it carried friendship and commiseration over the recent losses to cancer of Rosetta's husband and Leah's own mother.

Dressed in her usual long skirt and knitted top, her eyeglasses sliding down her nose, Rosetta was a quiet woman, with the same lean, strong build as Anna. Usually taciturn, she rarely spoke, but since her husband Ugo had died, she sometimes teared in emotional moments. If she forfeited these few tears, they were her only overt concession to grief. Like her own mother before her, Rosetta too had trimmed grapevines, planted and harvested a vast garden, butchered in season, cleaned, and cooked. With always the same quiet joy, she was the one who had taught Anna to work, and now in her seventies, she still worked alongside her daughter, matching the younger woman's pace.

Carla, Leonardo's mother, came to hug Leah last, stepping forward from where she had been standing on the opposite side of the kitchen leaning against the lintel. She was the grandmother from town, who like the others had worked all her life but was now frustrated by macular degeneration. Her gift, which she carried into the threatening dark of blindness, was telling stories. She could recount dozens of tales, memories from her childhood, folktales her parents had told her on winter nights, and anecdotes from life in Scansansiano and the countryside. With graceful gestures, she spun the stories out in great detail at the extended weekend meals, teaching Francesca and the others their history, their culture.

A thin, graceful woman, Carla's hands moved incessantly, fluttering like little birds. Stories over, she brushed crumbs from her lap, picked a bit of lint from Francesca's shoulder, or rubbed one hand over the other as her hands tried to settle in her lap.

In her early eighties, Carla's memory was keen. Leah remembered how she recalled an incident from World War I, when the women and children had made a procession out of town, down the steep hillside, across the bridge spanning the river and up the rough dirt roadway toward the Church of Santa Maria to pray for their husbands, fathers, and brothers.

As they passed under the sheer tufa wall below the church, the rock face had given way. Huge boulders rumbled down onto the procession in a thick river of rock and boulder, crushing fifty-one women and children before cascading into the valley below. The screams of the mothers and wives and children had been lost in the thunderous downpour of rock.

Finishing the story, Carla brought her hand to her mouth, covering her lips, shaking her head slowly from side to side.

"That's the reason for the cross and those columns that rise up from the tangle of vines and brush at the roadside. Almost everyone has forgotten, but I remember, and the others that escaped remember."

She paused.

"It was as bad as when the Americans bombed the piazza and killed ninety-one of us." She sighed. "What's done can't be undone. The bomb had gone astray." She had said it in pure grief, without rancor, shaking her head slowly from side to side, while she gently whisked bread crumbs from the table with one thin white hand into the palm of the other.

Chapter Nineteen

Francesca took Leah by the arm. "Come see the pastries."

Leah glanced at Anna.

Anna patted her shoulder. "I know you want to hear about Giulio. Leonardo will tell you about it later. Go with Francesca and see the food. Take pictures for Nick's research, or maybe for a new article." She smiled sadly and tilted her head toward the other room.

The living room, originally the family's cantina with great barrels of wine on a raised portion of the floor and sausages and prosciutto hanging from the ceiling, had been renovated. With the addition of a back bedroom and bath, behind the new living room, Ugo and Rosetta could be on the ground floor.

Now a large oak breakfront stood at the far end of the room, away from the double-door entryway, through which the various troupes of the Befanata would enter as they made their rounds throughout the night. Tables at the sides of the breakfront were laden with deviled eggs topped with a swirl of red and white mayonnaise and a bit of black olive. There were dishes of home-cured olives from the Antonini's own trees and plates of uncured Tuscan salami, *soppressata*. There were sandwiches, a few pizzas, and a medley of desserts.

Leah pointed at one of the desserts, long rectangular pieces of brittle pastry covered with powdered sugar. "What's this one?"

"*Cenci* or *frappe*. We always have them for the Befanata."

"I thought frappe was a drink."

They both laughed. Francesca explained, "Maybe so, but it's also these

63

cookies, or *cioffe* or *chiacchiere* or *bugie*, or 'nothings.'"

"And this?"

"*Crostata di ricotta.* And those two," she pointed, "are *crostate* as well, apple and another ricotta, but not sweet."

And that big rectangular cake? The one covered with hundreds and thousands?"

"Hundreds and thousands?" Francesca wrinkled her nose.

Leah laughed. "The colored sprinkles. I translated it directly from English. I don't know the Italian."

"I don't know the Italian either. But the cake is very, very good!"

"I can't cut into that, but *castagnole!*" She pointed at another plate, took one of the golden round balls of pastry covered with powdered sugar, and raised it to her mouth. Realizing what she was doing, red with embarrassment, she stopped herself, hesitant to put it back because she had touched it.

"Sorry! I didn't think. They just looked so good!"

Francesca laughed. "Eat! That's what they're for."

Leah popped the sweet ball of dough into her mouth.

"Mamma!" Francesca shouted, laughing, "Leah can't stop herself. She's eating the castagnole!"

Anna's voice carried the lilt of laughter. "Tell her to have *schiacciata* as well. It will put a little meat on her bones."

"Foccacia?" Leah asked; she looked to Francesca.

"That what *you* call it, but it's a little different." Francesca responded, with a laugh.

Leah left the temptation of the desserts and returned to the kitchen just as Leonardo stepped through the doorway. She noted his haggard features, which reflected grief, dismay, and a gentle concern for his family. A handsome man approaching his fifties, he, like his wife Anna, exuded integrity, grace, and kindness. Leah felt again the great gift of having him and the rest of the family for friends.

Leonardo nodded in greeting to them all, then reached for Leah's hand.

"Hello, Leah."

"I'm sorry about Giulio. I know it's been a shock."

"A great shock." He passed his hand over his face as if to erase the vision of Giulio clawing the air. "We'll talk about it later."

He turned to Anna; there was a brief glance between them. "I think now, I need to get cleaned up, yes?"

"Yes. It's almost time," she said gently. "I've laid out your clothes."

Chapter Twenty

"Me? I never hunt cinghiale in the day—or under the full moon." Italo glanced at Nick for the hundredth time to make sure Nick was listening, then took the curve at full speed, swinging into the other lane, narrowly missing an oncoming car. The driver of the car laid on the horn, but Italo ignored it.

"During the day, or with the light of the moon? That's baby stuff! I wait for a moonless night, and I never shoot until I'm as close to the boar as I am to you now."

Nick emitted a little burst of air. He felt as if he were riding in a car full of mosquitos and silently cursed the fact there had been no room in one of the other cars.

Determined not to miss the only night of the year he could join the Befanata troupe, he had been determined to come but felt conflicted. The knowledge that Leah was in danger gnawed at him, and Italo's bragging exacerbated his unrest.

"If you look in the trunk you can see my rifle; it's a beauty. I'll show you."

"I thought you couldn't carry guns in the car."

"You can, with permission, but I don't pay attention. That law's for sissies!"

Nick grimaced. He wondered about Italo's friends. Who were they? Those who had met earlier to begin the rounds of the Befanata appeared to know Italo but not well. Nick had seen him often in the bar in Scansansiano, but he knew Italo didn't live in town. How did he get here? Why?

A handsome man with green eyes and wispy dark blond hair, Italo was generous in the way of offering drinks and meals, and he was a great storyteller and dancer. Nick remembered seeing him dance in the bar and was reminded of professional dancers on American TV. He exuded a superficial, initial allurement, but once out of sight, he was forgotten until the next time he twirled across the dance floor or offered drinks.

Suffering the drone of Italo's voice, Nick understood why Italo was tolerated but not befriended. He felt a headache coming on.

Angelina, Italo's girlfriend, befuddled Nick. No more than twenty-five at most, and maybe younger, she seemed much older. Average height with pockmarked skin, wide-set eyes, an oddly aquiline nose set in a squarish face with wide lips, her appearance was unsettling, like a puzzle the pieces of which didn't fit together. She was rough, metaled, and angry at everyone and everything.

While the first troupe members stood in the piazza waiting for the others, Nick had been introduced to her. Surprised by Angelina's strident voice and tough manner, Nick found communicating with her was a challenge. It didn't take long to understand it wasn't her appearance, strange as it was, that distanced people; it was her contrary attitude. Intent on keeping the conversation neutral and pleasant, he suggested the storm that had been predicted might not come. She countered, "Yes it will!" When he expressed his excitement over traveling with the troupe, she responded, "Something will go wrong, as usual." She disagreed with even the most neutral opinions, yet clung to the conversation as if it were food for a starving person. She pushed him away, but wanted to keep him, and more, it felt as if she were trying to pry information from him.

"Where's your wife? What work does she do? How much money can you make at that? Do you guys have children? What do they do? Is that good pay?"

Nick reminded himself to be generous. She had been patient and helpful, explaining to him how the main characters of the Befanata, the Befano, and the Befana, were two men who disguised themselves in advance in women's clothes, masks, and heavy makeup. He knew this from his research, but he saw that Angelina, when explaining and not complaining, had a gift for detail, for precise description. Still, when he saw the others stepping into the cars, he was glad to interrupt her and scuttle away with a hurried gesture.

To Nick's surprise, the first farmhouse was close to the road and renovated, a *casa colonica* modernized, complete with a swimming pool to the side. The outside steps leading to the living quarters on the second story had been rebuilt with fine travertine.

Nick had anticipated seeing the old *case coloniche*, with cows on the first level and living quarters above. Seeing this house, he stifled a laugh at his own fantasies.

Tumbling out of the cars, the motley members of the group drifted toward the steps, singing the traditional Befanata song, one but separate, their voices preceding them into the night air. Nick took note of the huge picture windows of the house, an American innovation. The troupe, Befana and Befano in front, musicians next, and the rest of the group behind, squeezed into the narrow stairwell and clambered together up the stone steps.

The owner of the house waited to open the door until they had gathered at the top of the stairs, then ushered them into the large sitting room with a haughty, peremptory manner that surprised Nick and the others.

Three small plates of store-bought cookies had been placed on one edge of a table near the doorway, and there were two inexpensive bottles of wine and a few plastic glasses sitting behind the cookies. Only one of the bottles was opened.

None of this was what Nick had imagined.

The family and their two friends had gathered at the far end of the kitchen, away from the door, and stood staring at the troupe, leaving them to chat amongst themselves.

Without even a tap of their feet when the music began, the family watched the dance of the Befano and Befana, as if observing, without interest, a play on stage. Andrea picked up the tempo and played louder, hoping it would incite the family to participate, to take joy in the tradition, and make a special effort. But the family remained apart, and the music faded.

Silvio, dressed as the Befana, walked what seemed to him the long distance to the end of the room and asked the husband of the household to dance the traditional Befana and host dance. Instead, the host pushed his teenage son forward.

After much cajoling, the boy reluctantly agreed, with a sour, resigned look on his face. As the last note sounded, he broke away and rushed back to the end of the room to join family and friends.

The reticence of the family infected the Befanata troupe, and the singing dwindled to a desultory murmur.

Andrea turned to a friend. "We need Giulio."

Italo, who had overheard, snapped, "I bet you're glad. You're next in line to inherit the cantina and that stupid collection of photos."

Andrea hissed. "Shut up! You don't know anything about it. And it's you who cares so much. You wanted Giulio to sell you the cantina for a restaurant. What a joke!"

Andrea raised his hand to strike Italo, but by an act of will, lowered his fist, spun on his heel, and stormed out the door.

At the other end of the room, the daughter of the family laughed with her friends at the two men, and stern-faced, her father rose, walked through the group to the door and stood, issuing by his stance and hand on the door handle, a silent invitation for the troupe to leave. Led by Silvio, the troupe slowly filed through the door, descended the steps, and crossed the grassy expanse of yard to the cars.

Chapter Twenty-One

Italo told Nick that he came from a village near the coast. From what he said, Nick understood Italo usually came to Scansansiano only for the holidays. When they had first been introduced in the broad expanse of the piazza, Italo had appeared to Nick to be a friendly, talented talker, an ideal informant for a folklorist. He had described in detail to Nick his farm near the coast, his business as an appliance salesman. His Italian was clear, educated, and sadly, Nick thought, without a trace of the local dialect.

Nick's hopes of an interesting discussion with Italo about the Befanata were quickly dispelled. Once back in the car, his questions were repulsed; Italo had bolted into a tirade of gossip about the town and the locals.

"People here don't understand business. They have no ambition, tradition yes, ambition no. And people would come for that tradition; they would *pay!* But these bumpkins don't understand that, or even if they do understand, they don't have the drive to capitalize on it. If there were a good, really good, restaurant, people would come from Rome and Florence just to eat here."

Nick protested. "There are excellent restaurants here – and people *do* come from Rome and Florence on the weekends."

"I mean *people*, important people. Like the ones Angelina works with in the ministry, the upper echelons. You know, *real people?*"

"Angelina works in the ministry? I thought she was studying real estate."

"She is, but she also does some secretarial work for one of the ministers."

"How...?"

"How'd she get that kind of work?" Italo laughed. "She's no dummy. And she has a hold over her father. He used to know the guy when they were younger, and he got the guy to give her some work, the filthy bastard."

"She's your girlfriend?"

"You could call her that, but my wife and kids wouldn't like it." He turned to Nick and winked.

"Your wife and kids!"

"What makes you think I wouldn't have a family?" Italo blurted out, insulted.

"But…"

"My wife does what I tell her to do. Besides, she knows Angelina."

"Incredible, and she…"

"And nothing. She's full of hot air; she won't do anything." Italo went on, imitating his wife, "You keep her away from here, from our family and friends, or I'll kill her!" He laughed. "She won't do anything, of course. She's a little mosquito; she buzzes and irritates, but that's all there is to it."

"What about Angelina; does she know about the marriage, the kids?"

"Of course! I told you! They went to school together." He laughed again.

Italo seemed to Nick to be always laughing, with a cynical stutter, about the emotional convolutions he'd created.

"And when Angelina is angry, she says the same things as Sophia. 'I'll kill her if you bring her here, if you make fun of me.' But she won't. Their families know each other, and I think they actually like each other. If it weren't for me, they'd probably be best friends."

Italo grinned with satisfaction. "Angelina is more of a wasp than a mosquito."

He paused, "You know Nick, you pay for love with pain, that's for sure. I can't tell you the troubles I've had—and there isn't any love without jealousy. Wow, if I had any wife but Sofia…"

"What if the wasp and the mosquito join forces?"

"They're not going to. They're both de-vo-ted!"

"Do you know what 'hubris' is?"

"No. What?"

"Never mind. I just wondered."

Anxious to keep attention on himself, Italo let it pass, a devilish grin on his face. "I think Angelina would lick my boots if I asked her," he grunted, "and I know for a fact she'd...." he punched Nick on the arm. "Don't tell me you wouldn't like a little on the side, huh?"

"Are the Antoninis next?"

"Okay. Okay. No, they're not next. It's some people up near the via cava. They usually have a big spread at least."

Resigned to his fate, Nick let it go, and they rode for a few minutes in silence. As crass and boring as Italo was, Nick guessed he must be a successful businessman; he wore a subtle, but very expensive, dark green suit cut and tailored in the dress style of the Roy Rogers films of the 1950s. The little boy cowboy.

Italo broke into Nick's musings. "I saw you two talking. She'll be in town tomorrow night."

Confused, Nick asked, "Angelina?

"Yeah. She's got some kind of real estate test. She'll never make it. People don't like the way she looks. She can only do the ministry job because she works from home. And real estate isn't what she's best at if you get what I mean. You know about her dad, right? He's always beating her. She likes that rough stuff, but it leaves her all bruised." His face contorted in an ugly grin. "But, hey, she thinks I'm a god and should have whatever I want, so who's complaining?" He worked his hands back and forth on the steering wheel.

"Her dad beats her?"

"God, yes. He beats her every chance he gets, and that's not all."

"Why does she stay? Why not report him? Why don't *you* do something?"

"What do ya think? That we haven't? Giovanna and I aren't idiots. We've talked to her until we're blue in the face, but she won't press charges, and she won't move out."

"Why?"

"Who knows? It's her business." He shrugged and leaned to the door as he took another curve.

Chapter Twenty-Two

Prating on as fast as he drove, Italo moved from his love life to his hunting exploits on the trail of cinghiali.

Resigned to his fate, Nick willed himself to enjoy the night. No matter how obnoxious Italo was, he was a fine storyteller. It was the way of fieldwork, except most people were more pleasant than Italo. Ninety percent of the time fieldwork conversations covered the everyday, mundane aspects of life, but there was the 10 percent when a conversation became a window into unique cultural knowledge.

Nick maneuvered Italo back to the subject of cinghiali. "The hunt must be frightening. Those tusks…"

"Hell no. Most of them run away. I never hunt those; they're the dumb ones. I hunt the brave ones, who stand their ground. People around here don't get it; they go out for the meat. They don't even understand the sport of it, the challenge. You have to get on an equal footing with the animals. 'Even the odds' – that's how you say it, right?"

He made a loud guffaw, proud of his self-proclaimed prowess and for knowing the English term. "It's not for nothing that in this part of Tuscany you see MMSS on a coat of arms."

"MMSS?"

"Misery, malaria, sweat, and *sangue*. How do say it? Blood? Ours is a hard life that produces hard men. Blood, Nick. Blood. We do what we have to do to live!" Italo's face contorted in hatred.

"Your life's been hard?"

"Damned right! And I do what I have to do." He shouted, his hands nervous on the steering wheel.

"But the cinghali, it's important to get the meat too, no?"

"Of course! But the ultimate goal is enacting the ancient, courageous spirit of hunting. I can't stand hunting with someone who doesn't want it dangerous. It's the same in business. I hate wimps. Business is just like the hunt. Exactly the way people around here *don't* treat it. Not to speak poorly of the dead, but Giulio didn't get it. He was a pansy. He could have gotten his aunt to stop waffling on that cantina and sign it over to him long ago, but he didn't do it, he didn't press her. If he had I would have..."

"You would have?"

Italo yelled, "Nothing! Forget it! It's better the way it is."

Nick was confused and on edge. Italo had leaned forward and picked up speed, then suddenly slowed and settled back in his seat. He tried to laugh off his outburst. "Forget it, Nick. Take a look in the back seat." He poked his thumb over his shoulder. "See that hat?"

Nick turned to the back seat. "It looks like one of our western cowboy hats."

"One of *our* cowboy hats. And your cowboy hats don't have silver ornaments like mine. Much better than American hats. And way more expensive. It's a Maremma hat. You know about Maremma cowboys, don't you?" Italo asked, petulant.

"Of course..."

"Well, I'm a cowboy."

"I thought you sold appliances."

"I do." He scowled at Nick. "But I'm really a cowboy. Like my grandfather. You may know a little Nick, but you don't know it all. We were the ones who beat Buffalo Bill when he came here in the 1880s. He thought he'd just walk in and show up the local yokels! But we showed him." Italo shifted in his seat in agitation. "That hat cost me thousands and thousands of lira. Thousands and thousands! And I can afford it because I don't wait around like other people do. I go after what I want, damn it."

Italo's diatribe created a tingling sensation of fear at the back of Nick's neck. He considered what Italo had been saying, bragging about. Starting a new restaurant in Scansansiano when Giulio sold him the aunt's cantina, denigrating Giulio's business acumen. Nick regarded Italo now, gripping the steering wheel, chewing his lip in agitation. Was he capable of murder?" He would ask Leah to go over the murder scene again, but for now, he wanted to keep Italo as calm as he could. "Wasn't too lively at that last house, was it?"

"They think they're above everyone else. I said that stuff about Andrea because it's true. He wants those photos so badly he can taste it. Did you see how he stormed out? Forget it."

Italo seemed to be talking to himself. "I should have kept quiet. Andrea and I have never been friends. And those people at the house are cold fish. A generation ago they were street sweepers in Rome and now they're big shots because somebody died. Maybe somebody will die and leave me money! Maybe they're dead right now and the check is in the mail!" He burst into wild laughter. "They'll learn. Arrogance goes by horse and comes back by foot."

Nick sneezed to cover his own burst of laughter at the irony of Italo's words.

"They're Roman; they don't know anything about the traditions around here. For them, the Befana is dolls imported from China made to look like some American Halloween witch, not like our Befana."

Nick cringed. 'Our Befana!' Like Nick himself, Italo had known nothing about the Scansansiano Befanata until a year or two before.

"They go for an evening walk in Piazza Navona, all lit up for Epiphany, buy a cheap doll, and tell their kids it's the Befana. If they'd fed us better tonight and had livened up the evening with some dancing, nothing would have happened."

"Wait. Just a second ago you said 'they're not from around here'. I thought you weren't from around here either."

Italo ignored him. "Have you heard of Tiburzi?" He poked Nick in the shoulder. "You should have in your line of work, Mr. Bigshot."

"I've heard of him."

"But you've only heard the official story, the one from the stupid tourist books, right?"

"Not exactly."

They took another curve at high speed. Nick grasped the door handle, wondering if the car headed for a crash there would be time to jump into the thick foliage along the road. The edges of the forests whipped by in the headlights. Coming up like a shot behind the other four cars in front of them, Italo slammed on the brakes.

"Ok, Tibruzi!" He spoke as if he had finished the task of threatening their lives and could get on with his story.

Nick took a deep breath to slow his pounding heart and tilted his head against the headrest. Waiting for Italo to begin, Nick's mind wandered to Leah. Was she holding up under the strain of silence?

Italo burst into song.

> *He made the hearts of men tremble*
> *And gave bread to those in need*
> *Domenico Tiburzi was his name*
> *And in the sad and moonless night*
> *With his rifle strapped across his chest,*
> *He defied storms and luck.*

He held the last note, then laughed with a great roar and stepped on the accelerator. "It's too long for me to sing the whole thing. But what a man he was! In the end, he had a strange burial, half in heaven, half damned to hell. But if it wasn't Capitano Michele Giacheri who killed him in those bushes outside the little hideout in Farene, then who was it?" Italo asked, rhetorically. "He killed himself! He had too much courage and dignity to let himself be killed by a local policeman. Way too much! My great-grandfather knew him, and I don't mean 'knew *of* him,' I mean *knew* him. Tiburzi was too proud to die at the hand of some local yokel."

Italo's voice was exceptional. As crude, as arrogant as he was, Nick promised himself he would interview him at length once the murderer was caught and Leah was safe.

Seeing an opening in Italo's diatribe, Nick took his chance.

76

"Do you think Giulio killed himself?'

Italo grunted, "Giulio was a loser. He had no drive; he wanted to sing and wait for his inheritance from his aunt."

"The cantina? The photos?"

"Witch! She played those two like a fiddle, and they fell for it."

"Played? She'd finally decided."

"The gossip was she'd changed her mind with some other wacky plan just before she left." His voice turned angry. "What a bitch!"

"Who's the source?"

"What are you, a detective? Forget it!"

Nick made the connection. "It was *her* cantina you were going to buy!"

Italo turned toward him, "I said forget it! Who wants to waste time with those jokers anyway. Tiburzi was in another whole class. He knew what he wanted and he went for it."

Chapter Twenty-Three

At the second house, Nick stepped from the car, punched the record button on his tape recorder, and stepped to the front of the group to catch the song and muted sound of the troupe's feet crunching on gravel. Terzo, whom Nick had seen working in the electrician's shop, rang a cowbell to announce their arrival. Andrea and young Angelo, who worked in the grocery store just off the piazza in town, were playing their accordions. The butcher, Giovanni, strummed his guitar, his little son weaving back and forth in front of them, as they approached the house:

> *Good evening everyone,*
> *Tonight is the Befanata*
> *And in the name of Mary*
> *We come to greet you*

Rounding the corner of the house, the troupe found the owner of the farm standing at the wide-open doorway, smiling. Members of the household and friends peered from the doorway. As the song came to an end, they parted, and the host led the troupe into the dimly lit house.

Inside, Nick saw what the Befanata must have been like in earlier decades, perhaps in earlier centuries. The family and friends were gathered together: elders in black, children darting back and forth, babies crying and laughing, teenagers huddled in a group apart. Adding to the low electric lights, a fire danced in the grate at the back of the room, and the faces of the family glowed with joy and anticipation. A long trestle table was crowded with platters of homemade cakes, sausages, cheeses, sandwiches of tuna pate, biscotti, and bottles of homemade wine and grappa.

The troupe bunched inside, near the doorway, watching as the Befana and Befano stepped to the middle of the room and stretched their arms toward one another to open the dancing. Nick quickly set his tape recorder on a little table to the side and took the camera from his pack.

The musicians continued in a measured, stately tempo while the couple, in their droll costumes, danced in exaggerated motions in time to the music. A stanza or two in, the Befano and Befana broke to dance with the host and hostess and waved their arms, inviting others to join. The music picked up. Soon everyone but a few of the older people was dancing, stopping only now and then to eat and drink from the heavily laden table.

Two women in aprons stood in the doorway that led to the kitchen watching the festivities. Nick moved around the room snapping photos, stopping intermittently to transfer the recorder to another spot. He worked hard to concentrate, to capture the gentle chaos and vitality of the event, wishing the evening's joy were not juxtaposed with the murder.

As he worked, he caught a glimpse of Secondo, surprised to see him sitting amongst the family members. He thought of Secondo as the town orphan, if a man of 32 can be an orphan. He watched him sip his wine and chat with the wrinkled septuagenarian sitting next to him. Why was Secondo named Secondo if, as Leonardo had told Nick, he was an only child?

Secondo noticed Nick and waved. Nick returned the gesture, but even as he did, he wondered if Secondo, in one of his 'episodes' as the neighbor had called them, could be capable of murder.

An older man and woman, guests whom Nick had seen talking to Andrea, came to Nick with an offering of their wine and a tray of cheeses and cakes.

"American?" the wife asked in heavily accented English.

"Yes," Nick responded in Italian to put her at ease. "What a fine Befanata. Do you come to the family every year?"

"Yes!" A broad smile flashed across the old man's weathered face, wrinkled as apples. "For many, many years! After my father and mother were gone. They had had the celebration for many years, and my grandfather and grandmother too!" He laughed. "But we are friends here, so we have come here."

"You must know the history of this area very well."

"Oh, yes. But we never saw *your* countrymen until the war. We were hiding our Jews in the caves on our farm and were concerned with that. It was horrible evading the Germans. But one day there was a dogfight here, nearby, above the lower fields." He waved his arm toward the west. "An American plane was shot down. The pilot and copilot parachuted out. We could see the big mushrooms floating through the sky. Two of our neighbors got to them before the Fascists and the Germans, and they stayed here, in our caves, with the Jews. Real Americans. And later..."

The woman touched the man's arm, and he stopped mid-sentence.

Nick knew he was thinking about June of 1944 when an American bomber's system went haywire and instead of bombing German headquarters off the piazza in town, the bomb plummeted like a hawk toward the edge of the piazza, killing ninety-one townspeople.

The townspeople had understood, but the dead were dead. Nick realized this gracious man was of an age to have known many of them. The memory of that devastation showed in his eyes.

The old man continued without mention of the American bombing. "I've been to the American cemetery outside of Florence, and the small one at Assisi. Vast fields of crosses and Stars of David. All of them died trying to help us. Most of them were just boys, eighteen or nineteen years old. Like every war. I won't forget." His voice had faded to a whisper.

"Enough, Lonzo. It's the *Befanata*." Short and stocky, with strong hands and a generous, warm demeanor, the older woman gently laid her hand again on her husband's forearm, then turned to Nick and raised her arms, inviting him to dance. "You have to participate to understand, Signor."

Nick laughed. "Of course!" He laid his camera on the table and guided her into the dance.

Towering over the older woman by more than a foot, Nick jigged around the room, jostling, bumping along with the others to "Mamma, Mamma, I saw the Befana."

Nick noticed Silvio had taken up the camera from the edge of the table and was helping out by taking photos while Nick danced. On the heels of the closing notes, the musicians sounded the first strains of "Oh, Marina." The woman squeezed Nick's hand and moved away to pull another into the dance.

In the flush of his dance with the older woman, Nick experienced a regret that he had not yielded to Leah the few times she had asked him to take her to a dance. Uncomfortable with the jollity and physical expression of dancing, he had given in to his natural reticence and never taken her.

You have to participate to understand, the woman had said.

A half hour of dancing, eating, and drinking passed before the musicians struck the first notes of "Maremma Amara," a sad song followed immediately by "Scansansiano," a love song for the town and countryside. The ebullient mood of the first songs faded to a mellow reflective yearning, a collective love for place and way of life.

Just then, Nick saw Andrea move forward. One of the young women of the group draped her arm over his shoulder. Nick heard her say, "Don't let Italo get to you. He shoots his mouth off, but I don't think he really means it."

In the car again with Italo, Nick set his teeth for the ride to the Antoninis, the next stop. Staring into the darkness and the thick web of trees passing in a blur along the roadside, he thought with anticipation of the joy of the *Befanata*, of sharing that joy with friends. The event was also a chance in this long night to help alleviate the heavy truth Leah carried. When his mind wandered to the wizened and gentle couple he had met, the thoughts sobered him to realize anew that murder had wounded this strong sense of community.

Chapter Twenty-Four

Supper was quiet. Leah and the Antoninis were subdued by their own thoughts and grief. The trauma of the day had heightened Leah's attention to nuances. She glanced at each member of the family in turn and teetered on the edge of revealing what she had seen. She felt guilty holding back this information from good friends, but as she wavered, she remembered Nick's words. *They already have the steel weight of sadness on their shoulders. Don't add the shadow of murder now. The whole story will come to light later.*

Nick was right; they would understand. For this one, last night the Befanata could continue in the traditional way, not with an association to murder, but as a tribute to a man who had been a perennial and integral member of the local troupe. For years to come, there would be a fringe of sadness to the Befanata because of Giulio's death. But for this night, groups coming from outside areas would know nothing of Giulio or his death. It would be enough for Anna and Leonardo to host them, without the added burden of a new fear, of doubled grief and shock.

After the soup, as they were eating the main course, Leonardo, speaking in a near whisper, began the story of what he had seen. His handsome, weathered face was tense with emotion and effort, but his voice, by force of will, remained steady. He had been a schoolmate of Giulio, not a close friend, but the town was small and the two men often saw each other and spoke about hunting.

As he spoke, Leonardo created a vision of an inclusive community. In the endless round of school children becoming adults, marrying or not, succeeding or not, stumbling into drugs and dismay or not, Leonardo's vision and the vision of the town was that everyone belonged. If they did not always interact, or if they had committed some wrong, still they belonged, and people who could were ready to help. People who hadn't the means to help were ready to encourage, to offer work, to extend a hand on the trail back from trouble to balance.

Leah thought of Coretta Scott King: *the greatness of a community is measured accurately by the compassionate actions of its members.* This was Scansansiano.

A pained expression crossed Leonardo's face. The community had sustained terrible damage in Giulio's death. Others had died, of course, but the idea of suicide shredded the spirit of the town. People felt as if they had let Giulio down.

Leah emitted a soft ahhhhhh.

"What is it, Leah? What's wrong?"

Her face turned red with frustration at herself.

"Nothing. I'm sorry. Just a hiccup."

Francesa patted her back, and Leonardo went on.

"Anyway, this morning, since I had today and tomorrow off, I called the police to ask if I could bring my gun in the car to that area, and the Lieutenant gave permission...."

Leah looked puzzled.

Leonardo nodded his head.

"It's the law, Leah. We have to ask permission; it's not like America." His lips lifted in a slight smile.

Curious to ask him more about the gun laws, but hesitant to interrupt the story, Leah gave a brief nod and fell silent.

Leonardo continued, the soft "shh" sound of the Tuscan dialect more pronounced than usual.

"I was on the trail down river below the table rock, planning to meet a friend near the bridge, when I heard the scream."

He stopped to clear his throat.

"A few days ago, I'd run into Giulio in town, and he told me he'd seen cinghiali in the gorge a few days before. He was excited about going hunting himself and was planning to go out today. We laughed about maybe I would get all the cinghiali before he had a chance. He seemed happier than he's been lately. He said last week he'd talked to his aunt about her cantina, and he had hopes she was going to give it to him. That cantina! What a problem that's been, with promises back and forth. I hope Signora Seta will decide soon.

Tito was the first to sense something; he stopped and looked up. Then I heard the scream and looked up, and I saw a man flailing in the air. For an instant, I thought I was dreaming. It didn't make sense. And it seemed as if the falling would never end, yet it was only seconds.

He crashed through the limbs of the trees. The branches cracked and broke and then he hit with a terrible sound, a thud I'll never forget. Tito ran for him, and I followed through the brush. When I reached him, Tito was standing by him, sniffing. Giulio was face down, but I knew who it was, and by the posture, I knew he was already dead. His legs and arms were askew, and he was bleeding, but the worst was the way his neck tilted to one side, like a bird that has hit a window.

I tried to call Lieutenant Cavour, but there was no reception, so I sat by Giulio hoping someone would come by. It wasn't long before Guido came looking for me because I hadn't shown up at the bridge. I sent him up to town to call Cavour and show him the way.

Sitting next to Giulio, all I could think of was how happy Giulio had been about the possibility of getting the cantina, and how, when we were kids, he was always singing, like he sings—sang—for the Befanata."

Silence blanketed the room; each of them could feel death crowding next to the joyful Befanata festivities about to begin. Each of them sitting at the table had experienced personal or family tragedies, but as a suicide, this particular tragedy enveloped the whole family, friends, acquaintances, the whole town. The feeling they had somehow failed one of their own would pervade every activity and event for weeks to come.

Leah listened in restless silence as Leonardo continued.

"When the Lieutenant and Sergeant Gianicollo arrived, they paid little attention to Giulio. They told me to step away and not touch anything, so I called Tito to my side, and we waited. They stretched tape in a circle around the area, took photos…"

Leah moved uneasily in her chair. She was sweating and her face had flushed a bright red.

"Leah, I'm upsetting you," Leonardo leaned toward her.

"No, I'm fine!" She held her hands up, palms outward, as if, contradicting her words. "Please, go ahead. I'm just hot." She plucked at the sleeve of her sweater and shrugged out of it, twisting to drape it over the back of her chair. Francesca rose and moved around the table to open the front door a crack so the cold air could cool the room.

Leonardo continued. "I could hear them talking. There was something about the way Giulio had fallen that made them think he hadn't jumped, but that maybe he'd been pushed. I think maybe they were right. I don't want it to go beyond this family, but I don't think Giulio would have committed suicide. Ever. He was cantankerous, a fighter, generous in a particularly impetuous way even. He did get into drugs once he was out of the army, but he was still stubborn and always thought he was right. He used to argue, even over little things…" Leonardo smiled at the memory. It was Giulio's character to be obstinate, and I can't imagine he ever got depressed enough to do away with himself, even with the drugs."

"Who do you think could have killed him then?" Leah tried to make the question seem matter-of-fact, but coming unexpectedly, it sounded jarring, blunt, especially from Leah. Leonardo emitted a loud cough as if someone had struck him on the back. He reached for his glass and took a long drink of water.

"This is a difficult question. We can't think of anyone from our town who would have done this. We have drugs and affairs and some theft, but a murder happens maybe once in a hundred years, and usually, it's some outsider."

Leah had been indelicate, impolitic. Still, she pressed on. "Someone from outside?"

Leonardo hunched his shoulders. "I don't know. We can't know."

"From one of the towns around Scansansiano?"

"We know those people almost as well as we know ourselves. Who among any of us would want to kill Giulio? What for?"

Carla interjected. "And no one knows where Giulio's aunt is. They can't find her. She told me she planned to go to the coast to meet a friend from Rome, but she didn't say who it was or where they were staying, or even if they were staying on the coast. It's terrible she doesn't yet know and we all do. She'll be traumatized." She brushed at her skirt as if to dust off crumbs.

"Did you tell the police, Nonna?" Francesca addressed her grandmother.

"No police to tell. I asked, but one was out with the body and, like Leonardo said, the other one has gone to the provincial office. They'll be out for a few days, I imagine."

Chapter Twenty-Five

At the touch on her shoulder, Leah swung round with a shout.

"Leah! It's okay; it's just me."

In the impulse of protection, Anna hugged her. "I wanted to tell you they're coming. Driving in now."

Leah's face flushed. "I'm sorry. I've been concentrating on photos of the food I'll use for the article. I didn't hear you."

It was a lie; she shifted her gaze.

"You're nervous tonight, Leah. Is everything alright? Can I help?"

"I guess I'm more worried about the article than I thought I'd be."

"I thought it was about the vie cave."

"It is, but I'd like to add something about food too, and tonight's my chance for photos."

"What can I do to help?" Anna repeated.

"It's not just the food…it's this murder too."

"Don't say 'murder,' Leah. We don't know for sure."

"But…"

Anna read the fear in Leah's eyes. "What is it? There *is* something."

"I can't talk about it. Please." She grasped Anna's hands, "please."

Anna pulled her close. Leah could see by the look in her eyes she was wondering whether to press her for more, but Anna let it go. "Don't worry. You're safe with us. You don't have to say anything now, or ever. Just try not to think about murder, Leah. We can't know that, can we? The thought will only torment you."

Leah turned away. "Of course, you're right."

They passed into the next room and could hear the troupe singing as they approached the house. Leonardo opened the door, and with the whole family standing beside him, waited for the troupe to appear around the corner. Leah leaned forward, hoping it would be Nick's group.

When she saw him, she darted through the others, took his arm, and pulled him to the side, whispering, "Have you heard anything?"

Nick leaned toward her and muttered, "Not much. Try to let it go, Leah; you look so tired. Hang on; it'll just be a little longer."

The crowd gathered in a circle. Silvio and Giovanna, *Befano* and *Befana*, danced a few bars together, then drew Leonardo and Anna into the dance, swinging to the music. Soon others joined, and some pressed close to the table laden with the savory and sweets Leah had tasted earlier. Nick moved through the crowd snapping photos from various angles to capture the sense of motion and the faces of the troupe and hosts.

A man shouldered his way through the others and come toward Leah. He was a handsome man of average height with green eyes and wispy, dark-blond hair. Leah had stood next to him at the table and heard him bragging to a reluctant bystander. The woman excused herself saying she needed air.

Now, the man stopped in front of Leah and extended his hands. Leah stood still.

He made a face. "Well, would you like to dance?"

"Oh. The way you extended your hands and didn't speak, I thought you were asking for money or something."

"Money? Do I look like I need money? I want to dance." He was obviously miffed. Leah silently chastised herself.

"You're…?"

"Italo! Your husband's riding with me. You didn't know?" He made a face, as if she should have known.

"He mentioned you just now." She took his hand, and they moved onto the dance floor.

He was an expert dancer in the tradition of Gene Kelly and Fred Astaire: light, smooth. Leah's feet felt like stones; she barely managed to keep up. A bear dancing with a gazelle. His physical presence exuded an allurement, but once the dance and their brief, one-sided conversation was over, the enticement of his physical grace faded, and she understood he was nothing but a man full of himself.

"And the houses, so far?" Leah asked in politeness.

"What should I say? Not yet the most exciting Befanata. And riding with your husband? He's a little reserved." Italo bent his lips next to her ear. "But you don't seem reserved at all. I saw you run to him when he came in." He grinned lasciviously and pulled her roughly against him.

Leah pulled back. "He's my husband."

"But something new is always exciting, no? Let yourself go; it's the Befanata."

Leah dropped her arms and stepped away. "You're right, Italo. I should let myself go."

She turned and walked off the dance floor.

Anna came to stand by Leah. "Is Italo bothering you?"

"A buffoon. He's no bother."

"Be careful. He may be a buffoon, but he's a wily one." She sighed. "Perhaps it would have been better to cancel the Befanata this year. I think we're all feeling a little guilty to be dancing on the day poor Giulio died."

"I'm not sure. I think Giulio would have wanted it this way; having the Befanata pays tribute to him. Like the Irish wakes. We've been talking about him, telling stories, and I bet the members of the troupe have been doing the same in the cars."

Anna gave Leah a quick hug. "True. We're remembering him." She drifted away to a friend.

A woman Leah didn't know came to her side and took her hand. She spoke in a feathery voice. "Friends with the Antoninis?"

Leah, less than average height, looked down at the tiny little woman's rosy cheeks and frizzy gray hair. "Yes, for a while now."

"I remember seeing you in town."

"My husband and I are both here."

The woman's eyes glistened in the light from the fireplace. "I visit the Antoninis every year for the Befanata. We've known each other since we were children. And," she gave a mischievous smile, "Anna makes the best pastries in the area." She pointed at the cake, behind her. "Have you tried?"

"Not yet."

"Don't wait, or it will be gone—and don't let that Italo bother you. He's a bad one." She squeezed Leah's hand, turned to wave at a rotund little woman on the far side of the room, and moved away to speak to her.

"Second warning this evening," Leah muttered.

Chapter Twenty-Six

Giovanna called for a snake dance, and Leah stepped forward to join. Each dancer put hands on the shoulders of the one in front, and the snake wound back and forth in a sinuous figure-eight. Once they were gliding easily throughout the room, Andrea picked up the tempo. The rope of dancers kept pace, faster and faster about the room, heads bobbing from side to side, laughter rebounding from the white walls.

The song ended abruptly. Breathing heavily, Leah stepped aside to stand by Rosetta at the table of food.

"That's a beautiful hat Italo is wearing."

Rosetta nodded. "Yes, like your American cowboy hats. Many of the men have them, for work, but cheaper, not one so well made as that one."

"Another snake dance!" someone shouted.

The musicians took up their instruments and began to play at a frenetic, driven pace, as if the community wanted to force sadness from its midst and let tradition bridge the chasm Giulio's death had created.

Veering into a curve, skirting the dessert table, something flew out of Silvio's pocket and bounced off the wall into the middle of the floor.

Stefania, one of the young women of the troupe who worked as a clerk in the grocery store in town, stooped to pick it up. Seeing what it was, she yelled above the music. "Stop! This is Giulio's bullet necklace. The one he made in the army."

The music stopped abruptly. Hearing Giulio's name, the room went silent. Stefania was staring at Silvio. He glared at her, then swiftly stepped forward grabbing at her hands.

"Give it to me! It's mine." His words were warped by his Befano mask, which had twisted and slipped on his face, giving him the appearance of a misshapen devil.

Stefania stumbled backward, sweat trickling down her flushed face. "It's not yours. It's Giulio's. Everyone knows it. You may have served with him, but the bullet isn't yours. He told me he was going to give it to someone as a present, and he didn't mean you!"

Silvio tore off his mask. "Tell them!" he barked at Giovanna. Beads of sweat slid down his cheeks and dropped off the smooth line of his jaw.

Giovanna's costume had twisted. The mask she wore disheveled her hair. Makeup ran down her face. "Tell them what?"

Her eyes emanated cruelty. Riding a memory of her exchange with Giulio, she hissed. "That's Giulio's bullet. How did you get it, huh? He told me he'd never take it off, somebody'd have to kill him to get it. So, how'd you get it?" She circled her arm in the air, "Come on everybody, let's get to the next house."

Shocked to silence at what was said and the affront to the Antoninis, the group filed out behind Giovanna, with Silvio trailing at the end. Nick rushed to Leah, "I'll stay with the troupe, and see you back at the apartment?"

"Francesca's giving me a ride, go, go!"

Anna, Carla, Francesca, and Leah quietly straightened the trays on the table and began replenishing the buffet for the next group. Leonardo had gone out to watch the others leave. The women could hear Tito barking as the cars bumped down the rough lane and turned onto the highway.

Side by side with Carla, Leah set plates heaped with more sandwiches at the end of the table and dusted crumbs from the tablecloth into her hands. When Carla turned toward the kitchen for more food, Leah stopped her with a gentle touch on the arm.

"What was that scene with Stefania, Giovanna, and Silvio about?"

"Love and jealousy are born together, Leah. Giulio and Giovanna used to be lovers." Carla shook her head.

"But he was so much older."

Carla laughed sadly. "The ego never ages! And sometimes a girl looks for the parent they never had. Silvio is much older too, no? Giovanna's had a hard life. I don't know all the details. There are drugs, Silvio and Giulio in the army together, and I don't know what else…jealousy is like a civil war inside you; it ruins everything and makes people crazy."

Chapter Twenty-Seven

Leah and Nick bolted from bed when the telephone squealed the next morning at 9 a.m., 4 hours after they had returned to the apartment. Scrambling for the phone, Leah knocked her book and glasses off the nightstand.

"Damn it!" she shouted in a voice gravelly from sleep.

"Mom? It's me. What are you cursing about? And what's with the voice?"

Leah cleared her throat and ignored the mention of cursing. "Not much sleep, Sara."

"I thought dad would be up inputting his notes already."

"Not this time. Yesterday was exhausting."

"I thought the Befanata wasn't until last night. What was up yesterday?"

Leah ran a response through her mind. *Oh nothing, just seeing a murder, being pursued, hiding in the dust of a burial cave, trying to act normal, knowing I'm in the sights of a killer.*

"You know, preparation and I was taking some photos on one of the vie cave."

"Are you guys fighting?"

"No. We're fine. Does it seem like we're fighting?"

"You sound like you're trying to hide something. Your voice is all funny."

"We're fine. What about you two? Are you enjoying Paris?"

"It's Prague, Mom, Prague. And we've got news for you." Leah could hear the child in her voice. "We're coming to see you!"

"You're coming? Did you already buy the tickets?"

Leah turned to Nick and made a face.

"Gee, don't get *too* excited."

"I'm sorry, I…"

"Mom! Show a little enthusiasm. It's not all about the money. Cheap tickets if we came through Prague, and we had to grab them fast. Since we postponed the wedding we can afford it, so we're spending some time here and catching Czech Airlines to Rome. I wanted to surprise you, but Jonathan said I'd better not, just in case. And it sounds like it was a good thing I didn't." Sara was disgruntled.

"It's not that I'm not excited," Leah was struggling to find an excuse, "it's just…I haven't done anything about canceling the wedding. I haven't even called Genna. When will you come?"

"I'm not a baby, Mom. *I* called Genna, and between the two of us, we've cancelled everything. It's taken care of. And I'm not sure when we'll come." She giggled.

"Why are you giggling?"

"Nothing. Just happy to be talking to you." She broke into a full laugh.

"What is wrong with you? What's all the laughter?"

Sara had burst into uncontrollable hoots.

"Okay. Howl away. I won't ask again."

"We're…going…to poke…around Prague…for a little before…" She chortled.

"Yes, you said."

"Come on, Mom! You don't sound excited at all!"

"Just tired. We got in very, very late—or very, very early."

"Okay, listen, sorry I woke you, I've got to go, Johnny's waiting." She laughed again and hung up.

"Tell me," Nick grunted.

"They're in Prague, and they're coming here."

"Let's hope it's after all this is settled."

"With our usual timing? Not likely."

Chapter Twenty-Eight

The narrow streets of Scansansiano's old town were like the vie cave. On both sides of the walkways, apartment buildings of tufa rose high above Leah and Nick, blocking the sunshine. On the way to coffee and then the police station, they leaned into the slight upgrade, anxious to reach the bar that stood in the open sun on the corner of the piazza.

"Is there any way to stop them from coming?" Nick asked.

"We could tell them the truth."

"Then they'd come for sure."

"Let's hope for the best. Prague's an interesting, beautiful place. It'll probably be several days, if not a week. We'll deal with the police, and then what happens, happens."

Nick stopped and faced her. "And you will stay home and have nothing to do with it, right?"

Leah blushed. "You never told me what happened on the ride with Italo."

"My God!" He clasped his palms together and shook them up and down. "Okay, change the subject. But I'm watching. You have to let the police handle it. Now let's get coffee."

The bar was empty. Leah and Nick sat at the window table near the door. After a double espresso, Nick leaned back in his chair.

"Italo's a weird guy. Non-stop talker. And a braggart. He says he only hunts cinghiali at night, when there's no moon, and he never shoots unless he's—and I quote—'as close as I am to you now.'"

"Anna and a friend of hers both told me he's a wily one. They wanted to know if he'd been bothering me."

"Had he?"

"He's obnoxious, but not dangerous."

"Don't be too fast to judge. There's an underlying current of potential violence there. He fashions himself a real lover. Angelina's his mistress, and he's got a wife and kids in some village south of here. The guy couldn't stop talking about himself." Nick imitated Italo. "'His wife's a mosquito and Angelina's a wasp, but they know each other and everything is hunky-dory, and he's the king.' I asked him what would happen if the wasp and the mosquito join forces, and he said 'They're not going to. They love me too much. They're de-vo-ted! They'd lick my boots if I asked…' I asked him if he knew what hubris was."

Leah snorted.

"He also carries a gun in his car…"

"That's illegal."

"According to him, the law's for sissies. But the point is not that he's breaking the gun-carrying laws. It's that he's got a gun."

"Did you meet Angelina?"

"She was there with the troupe. I think she'd been helping with the make-up. Anyway, someone introduced us."

"What's your take on her?"

"Contrary. You know her, right. Squarish face, small, wide-set eyes. Maybe 'jagged' is the best word. Like a puzzle with pieces that don't fit. And contrary, geez! I mentioned it might rain, and she said it wouldn't. I told her I was excited to be traveling around with the troupe, and she said something was sure to go wrong, that it always did."

"You must have been glad to leave."

"More than." He hesistated. "She asked about you, too."

"Why?"

"You're a part of the gossip mill. A foreign woman in town."

Leah shrugged. "Did Italo talk about Giulio?"

"Yeah, but first he and Andrea got into it. It was bad. He heard Andrea say to one of the other guys that the group needed Giulio. That set Italo off, and he started yelling. He said he bet Andrea was glad, since Andrea was next in line to inherit the cantina and that he coveted that 'stupid' collection of photos. Andrea shouted back, called him a bastard, and said everyone knew that Italo wanted the cantina, so Italo should just shut up. I thought Andrea was going to hit him, but he just spun around and left. It was a desultory event anyway, and of course, after that, we had to leave."

"What about Andrea?"

"Nothing. We all left after him. He went with the others. As soon as I got in the car, Italo bolted into a tirade. He said he could never live here, that people here didn't understand business, that they have no ambition, tradition, he conceded, but no ambition. He ranted. People would come to his restaurant! *Real* people, and they would *pay!* Then he said people here were bumpkins who didn't understand, and they didn't have the drive to capitalize on possibilities. He insisted that if there were a 'good' restaurant, people would come from Rome and Florence just to eat here."

Leah laughed aloud. "They *do* come here to eat, and the restaurants are glorious."

I told him that, and he said he meant important people, like the ones Angelina works with in the ministry, the upper echelons."

"Angelina works in the ministry! I thought she was studying real estate."

"According to Italo, she does."

"How is that possible then to work in the ministry? She doesn't seem the type. All that metal!"

"She works from home, so the metal isn't a problem. Plus, from what Italo says, she has a hold over her father. He's molested her since she was 5 or 6, and she has proof hidden away. She's blackmailing him. What a bastard! 'Evil by his very nature,' if it's true. But she won't press charges, and she won't move out. Then Italo started in about Angelina and his wife again. Anyway, Angelina's coming for the *cenone*."

"What?"

"The cenone. The meal we'll make with the food we were given. Did you forget?"

"Just for a minute. So she's coming?"

"Yeah. He said she had a big real estate test, so she'll be here.

Leah's eyes had brimmed with tears."

"What's wrong?"

"I was just thinking about Angelina as a little girl."

"Should I tell you the rest later?"

"No, tell me now."

Nick went on. "Italo thinks Giulio may have been a wimp and unassertive about getting the cantina from his aunt. Evidently, there was the idea Giulio would have sold Italo the cantina! Italo wants it so bad he can taste it."

"Greed."

"I heard more from others in the group. Evidently, Giulio would have sold the cantina to Italo. From what I heard, the two were planning a Fumblerooski. Since Giulio was oldest and most likely to get both cantina and photos—I guess she didn't want to split them—he told Andrea when she chose him, he would give the photos to Andrea, and keep the cantina for himself. But this is where the Fumblerooski comes in: Italo offered him way over price for the cantina, so Giulio promised Italo he would sell the cantina to Italo, keep the photos for himself to sell—they're worth thousands and thousands—and let Andrea take the hindmost. I guess with the thought of all that money from Italo, Giulio got even more greedy and could get all the sooner to his girlfriend in Rome."

"The plot thickens."

"Enough for all needs, but not enough for greed. Well, anyway, possible motives. If Italo ever thought, or learned, Giulio would waver on their deal, he could be the one angry enough to kill him."

"Or, if Andrea heard about the Fumblerooski, then *he* could be the one angry enough."

"Don't forget Silvio! From what Carla said, Giovanna was cheating. So Silvio could have…"

"I didn't know she was sleeping with both of them. But she's for sure on drugs and it seems Giulio was the dealer. From what I hear, he's the only 'responsible' dealer in town."

"We need to let all this percolate. What else from Italo?"

I thought he was from Scansansiano, but he said he's from a village near the coast. It seems like he comes to Scansansiano only for the holidays. At first, I also thought he'd be an ideal informant. Standing in the piazza before we left, he described his farm in detail, vividly. He speaks in educated Italian and besides the farm, has a business selling appliances. He also wears an expensive suit. You saw it, right? Roy Rogers."

"So what have we got? A narcissistic cowboy who sells kitchen appliances and dances well, but wants to open a restaurant. Andrea, desperately counting on a pack of old, but *very valuable* photos for the love of them and for the financial security. Silvio, who found out his girlfriend, Giovanna, was sleeping with his best friend. Or Giovanna who, according to the woman in the bar, was seen desperately hunting down—I forget his name—some part-time dealer and was angry as hell. And why else would she be hunting for what's-his-name if it wasn't for drugs? None of them is too different in size, if you're looking up at an angle from 20 yards below."

Nick laughed. "Given your size, it would hard for you to say any of them are anything but tall!"

Leah punched him in the shoulder.

Chapter Twenty-Nine

Leah and Nick crossed the piazza and walked up the ramp guarded by two stone lions to the castle that had once belonged to nobility, but now served as the seat of the city government. Nick pulled on the giant iron-ring handle of the wooden doorway, and he and Leah stepped into a foyer, bare except for an umbrella stand.

On the other side of double glass doors, Signorina MacCleod sat at the police reception desk reading a magazine that displayed a beautiful redhead on the cover. The illustration was a perfect mirror reflecting the signorina's long red hair that frizzed wildly about her face and accentuated the smooth, unblemished skin of her neck and cleavage.

Hearing the doors open, she looked up. "It's you! Visas, no? Or...," she smiled wickedly, and continued in her smooth Whitney Houston voice, "have you come to confess a murder?"

Nick and Leah flushed. "Visas."

Signorina MacCleod laughed. "Of course visas. Why turn so red?" She stood, showing a long expanse of bare legs below a short black skirt that ended ten inches above the high-heeled black boots she wore on her unusually large feet.

"I will tell the Lieutenant. You're lucky to catch him; he's here only a few minutes. He's very busy with this murder business, or suicide, or accident, whatever it was."

Swinging her hips in sinuous motion for Nick's benefit, she crossed the floor and knocked on Lieutenant Cavour's door.

A tall, lean man in his mid-forties, with thick dark hair, chestnut eyes, and a mustache, Cavour was an imposing figure. He was not happy to see them.

"I'm sorry. Signorina MacCleod should not have shown you in. I have no time to spare for visas today." He glared at the signorina. She failed to notice and returned to her desk.

Nick glanced over his shoulder. MacCleod had left the door ajar. He stepped back and gently closed it. Cavour watched, curious.

Leah leaned over Cavour's desk, speaking in a low voice.

"We've come about the murder."

Cavour straightened with such force he felt one of his neck muscles seize. Too dignified to show the pain, he controlled himself with difficulty and slowly raised his hand to massage his neck. "Murder? What makes you think it was murder?"

"I know it was murder; I saw it."

For an instant, Cavour's reserve faltered. "Santa Madonna! Sit down!" He cleared his throat, straightened his uniform jacket, and leaned back in his chair. "Speak!"

Leah described her walk up the via cava, how she found the place for a perfect shot below the table rock, how the camera had delayed a fraction and she had photographed the murder, then fled to the necropolis, down the dromos into the last cave, how she had jumped out at the killer, and how Nick had whistled and the killer escaped.

Finishing, she drew a long breath, sweat beading at her temples.

Furious, the Lieutenant hissed. "You jumped out at him? *Mio Dio*, Signora! *Cosa stavi pensando? Sei pazza o semplicemente stupida?* And why, for the love of God, didn't you come yesterday!

"Okay, I wasn't thinking clearly, but I'm not crazy or stupid. And we did come. You were out, and you were out when I stopped again on the way to the Antoninis, and you didn't answer your phone. Plus, the note on the door of the station said you wouldn't be in."

The Lieutenant grumbled, "Do you have the camera with you?"

Leah handed him the camera and plug. "You can upload it to your computer. The photo is the last but one, just click 'mode'."

He made a face. "I'm familiar with cameras, Signora."

He pressed the power button. A photo blossomed on the minuscule screen. He clicked once on the left side of the dial to find the previous photo. The murder appeared.

"It's too small to see here of course. I'll bring it up on the computer and enlarge the figures."

It was a dismissal.

"But...," Leah's voice held a kernel of anger; Nick intervened.

"But we need to make sure Leah's safe. Everyone, including your secretary, thinks we're here with questions about our visas, and we don't want anyone else to know the real reason. We need to quash any rumors about her being on the trail this morning.

"Do I look like an amateur to you, Signor Contarini?"

"No, but..."

"Good. Then you will understand that I know how to protect my witnesses."

He stopped himself, allowing his generous, gentle nature, generally hidden under the cover of his uniform, to break through the tough exterior he had constructed for his position as head of police.

"No one else, and particularly Signorina MacCleod—he indicated the door with a slight tilt of his chin—will know about this. Let me suggest that you stick to your research on the Befanata and enjoy the cenone. The two of you can take time to read a few more books in the safety of your apartment, and I'll have one of my men pass by a few times on their rounds to check on you."

Nick and Leah spoke at the same time.

"How did you know about my research?"

"I'm not a dog to be put in a kennel!"

The Lieutenant smiled. "This is a small town, Signor, and it's my business to know things. Everyone that rents to foreigners fills out paperwork for our office; you yourself filled out this paperwork."

"But I only wrote research."

"As I said, this is a small town. How could you imagine you would blend in? To use your American expression, 'You two stick out like a sore thumb.' Don't worry. It's a fine thing you're studying the Befanata."

He looked at Leah, a condescending smile on his lips. "But you, Signora, are a problem. You go too often and too early to the trails, and you will only get more trouble if you continue. I ask you to stay home, off the vie cave." He wiggled his finger at her. "Your magazine can wait, I think."

"My magazine *cannot* wait, and *I* cannot wait to find out who wants to kill me. Please bring up the photos now."

"Signora. This is police business, not yours! And certainly not for foreigners. I'll see you to the door."

Leah would not be dismissed.

"This, Lieutenant, *is* my business. It's my life the killer is after. C'mon Nick!" She cast a hard look at the Lieutenant, turned, and stalked to the door. The magazine could wait, the Lieutenant was right, but she would walk where she wanted to walk.

Chapter Thirty

At first light the following morning, Leah slipped from bed and tiptoed into the bathroom. Fumbling in the dark, she pulled on her jeans, shirt, and sweater, and bent to take her socks and shoes. By the door, she picked her jacket off the hook and stepped into the early morning air, closing the door gently behind her. She exhaled a long breath and sat on the little stone bench beside the door to put on her socks and shoes.

Halfway up the narrow street, she stopped to peer into the dim light of the little piazzetta. In the darkest corner, she saw Secondo lying on a bench, covered with his sleeping bag and blanket. He seemed to be resting easily. She continued to the piazza and the head of the trail that descended to the river, the highway, and across the meadow to the vie cave.

The morning was overcast and chilly, Leah's perfect weather. The night had softened; first light spread a gray cast over the piazza, over the fields and the sheep huddling in the corner of a green pasture on the hill across the river.

Leah zipped her sweater to her chin and started down the trail, content to be alone, to have space, away from other people to think and move as she wanted. She kept to a fast pace, driven by her own chemistry and recalcitrance combined with the desire to find some sort of clue to the murder.

The Lieutenant had offended her sense of independence. Every aspect of her being rebelled against being told what to do. There would be a dropped pen, a coin, something with fingerprints. Something.

Remembering an incident from her childhood, she smiled, wishing she could tell her mother that she had never changed, that she was still hardheaded, impetuous, stubborn. With a mix of joy and concern, her mother would have understood that the three-year-old Leah was a foretaste of Leah the woman. She hoped her mother would have been pleased, despite the troubles. Leah remembered.

Left for the first time to play by herself in the yard on a late spring afternoon, her mother had closed the gate, knowing Leah would be safe in the yard while she worked in the garden at the side of the house. The imprisonment infuriated Leah. She threw herself to the ground, kicked, screamed, and beat her fists. Her mother came from the garden; seeing Leah was not hurt, she left and closed the gate a second time; and a second time, Leah threw herself to the ground screaming. Again, her mother came to hold her, but Leah batted her away.

When her mother disappeared around the corner of the house, Leah toddled to the gate, climbed up, and flipped the latch, emitting a delighted squeal at how easily the gate swung open with her on it. An hour later, when her mother came again, Leah was playing happily in the yard, the gate wide open. From then on her mother, in an uneasy, unspoken agreement with Leah left the gate open.

The trail was wet from the morning's heavy dew, and the dark water of the river purled over rocks, plashing from bank to bank as it twisted in its bed toward the Tyrrhenian Sea. Leah descended rapidly toward the bridge, up and over the highway, and down again to the mouth of Via Cava San Raffaello.

Remembering the 'Gate Incident,' Leah thought of a letter she'd found on a visit home. It was from her mother to a friend.

You asked about Leah. What can I tell you? Leah is one of those buoyant, excited women, curious, always on the lookout for adventure. Her energy, from childhood, has been boundless, exhausting. I sometimes think of her as a child still. You know how children from sitting still will jump up and run, and from running stop abruptly, tumble into a chair exhausted, then, in the next instant, jump up again? Leah's like that, as if she has a bottomless reservoir of energy and readiness.

But I don't want to mislead you. Part of Leah is a dark country, a sort of hidden continent of which few people are aware. Nick knows and Sara knows. Sara once expressed it to me as an unexplored corner of her mom's fervid heart. She said she thought a woman so open to the splendor of the world is, willing or not, vulnerable to the shadows as well.

That's all Sara said. She was trying to be gentle, gracious. She loves her mom and didn't want to say more of the raw reality of living with Leah's intensity. And I didn't want to push it. We all have a darkness. Most of us ignore it or hide it; but under that bright exterior, Leah is always exploring that shadow part of herself. I think she thinks about it too much, but I give her credit for the courage to delve into her darker side. Most people won't do it. The point is, there are times she can't stop herself, but she is cognizant enough to know what she's like and who's hurt, and is getting more control with time, I think.

Both Nick and Sara decided to endure the aberrations of Leah's darker side and leave her to love them in her own vivid way, which is mostly a joy and her 'real' character, I think. She never intentionally creates trouble. That odd fissure in her heart is an imperfection, a black hole that sucks her in and attracts all sorts of troubled people—thieves and murderers, who then leave their kill at her feet.

Remember the political killings in Africa, when the authorities dragged the bodies through the street? The honor killing of that young girl in Central Asia? The 'accidental' drowning in a gravel pit in Switzerland? Leah was perilously involved in those incidents. She's gotten through so far, but if the past is any indication, I fear someday that dark corner in her chest may swallow her, like those wild rat snakes in Africa that eat themselves. Not a pretty analogy, but what is the best analogy for a complex, charming woman who too often does herself no good?

Maybe the best way is to think of Leah as a woman full of love whose karma keeps setting her in the middle of murders.

Finding the letter had relieved Leah and given her peace. Her mother articulated with love, that she knew her child, knew the good and the bad and loved her still. This had given her some peace as if a secret were finally in the open.

To enter the vie cave was to find another peace. Solitude, silence, and the crisp silver air of predawn. She was meant for this as much as she was meant for the turbulent, passionate love she shared with Nick and for the intense, fanged protectiveness she felt for Sara.

To be alone in nature was a gift beyond measure that her mother, restricted by her social milieu, had never attained, but who had encouraged Leah in her wanderings in the fields and streams from the time Leah was 6 years old. Her mother had taught her curiosity for the world around her and the courage to be alone. Leah remembered her mother sitting at the window, staring out over the dawning of the new day, relishing a few minutes of peace, the vision of the land before her. When Leah wandered along the river, she felt she was taking her mother with her, giving the older woman something she had longed for.

Leah's father was the same. "Look," he would say when on occasion they walked in the fields together. A bull snake. We'll put him in the bin to keep the mice down." He picked up the snake in two hands and they carried him back to the bin. "The hawk is angry with us," her father laughed, "he's young, he wanted this snake, but I got him first! Do you know what it means, Leah, when you see a hawk flying with a snake in its talons?"

"What?"

"It means pay attention to what's happening around you."

Leah was quiet; a story was coming.

"A long time ago," her father continued, "a poet named Homer wrote a book called the *Iliad*. It's about a war between the Greeks and the Trojans. Someday soon you'll read the book and Homer's other great story, the *Odyssey*, but for today, while we have the snake in our hands, I want to tell you the Trojans lost the war, and part of the reason they lost was because one of their great warriors, Hector, was told that an eagle carrying a snake had dropped the snake...." He looked down at his daughter. "Why? Because the snake bit him. Hector didn't pay attention, even though in ancient times that was an omen telling him he'd better stop and think about what he was doing. A good advisor, Polydamas, told Hector he should pay attention and should call off the attack. The omen was telling him he should wait. But he didn't wait."

Leah was silent. She listened hard to her father's story; she wanted to be like him, to be silent and strong, and most of all patient. But even at nine years old, she knew she would never be like him.

She sighed. If she had to keep moving, at least she spent her time moving in the natural world. At least she had inherited that part of her mother's and father's love and character.

A breeze awakened the trees and brush, and the birds began a gentle concert of sound. Leah smiled; it was a pleasure to remember her mother and father, and a torment to remember their sadness. Leah hoped the bright soul she had been as a child had been a solace to both her parents. She raised her hand and held high the ring her parents had given her, as if showing it to them. She was the product of their complexities. Since, only Nick had been able to understand and delight in her mix of illness and character.

A branch snapped. Leah stopped and swung around. She was a few yards from reaching the table rock, where she hoped to find something that would indicate the killer.

"Hello?" She called, peering into the murky air of the trail, kicking herself for not concentrating on where she was or on the sounds around her.

Secondo stepped out from a slight curve in the trail below her.

"Secondo! Are you following me?" Her voice half anger, half fear.

"Yes." He spoke matter-of-factly as if it were normal for him to be following her. "You sound mad."

"I am! You scared me. Why are you following me?"

"You're still mad."

"Why are you following me, Secondo? Answer me."

"Because you're not very smart."

Leah burst out laughing. "What do you mean? Why do you think I'm not smart?"

"Because you come out here alone, when it's still dark, and somebody got killed here, and you should know enough not to come here alone."

"Got killed?"

"Yes."

"How do you know Giulio was killed."

"I just know, and you shouldn't *be* here."

Leah stepped back, alerted by his suddenly threatening tone. This was an omen. "I think you're right, Secondo. And I will go back to town now."

"You shouldn't *be* here!"

Leah took a deep breath and exhaled slowly.

"Tell me what you're worried about, Secondo. I want to know what you're thinking."

"I'm not thinking anything except you shouldn't be here. Don't treat me like I don't know anything!"

"I'm not. I just wondered why. But it's not important; you don't need to explain. How about if I walk past you and go back to town right now?"

"Yes."

He stood his ground.

Leah judged the room she would have to pass in front of him. Three feet. She took a deep breath and let it out slowly.

"Ok. I'm going to go back to town now."

She walked slowly toward him, keeping her eyes on his, passed him by, and continued at a slow pace down the trail, listening for footsteps behind her.

Chapter Thirty-One

"You can't keep going there! What do you know about Secondo, really? Nothing! You don't know if he's capable of violence."

Leah took Nick's arm. "Calm down. You don't need to involve the whole piazza."

Nick glanced at the men sitting by the bar and lifted his hand in a feeble wave.

"Come on, Nick. Let's just get our coffee and go home to get ready for the cenone."

"How in the hell am I supposed to concentrate on the cenone when you won't listen to me or to the Lieutenant."

They stepped into the bar and took the table near the window. Leah sat quietly, distracted, chastised, but determined.

"I can see the wheels turning, Leah. Don't do it."

"Don't do what?" Leah loved him, his thick hair, his bright eyes, the way he loved her. Still there were times she wished herself away, back on the trails.

"I'm involved, Nick. I saw the murder. I'm involved, and I want to do something. You know I don't—can't sit around and wait for other people. You *know* me."

"I do know you. You've given me the worst pain and greatest pleasure I'll ever know. But Leah, Sara..."

"Don't Nick. You're thinking earlier times. Sara's grown now. I can't turn the clock back, and I've made whatever peace I can make with her—and with you. But making peace doesn't mean I can be somebody else. I'm better, I have more control, but I can't be somebody else. Just love me the way I am."

Nick took her hands in his. She could feel his warmth.

Chapter Thirty-Two

At the station, Cavour buzzed Signorina MacCleod. "Get Montaro on the phone and tell him to come to the office, now!"

"What shall I tell him it's about?"

"You don't need to tell him it's about anything. Just tell him to get over here now!"

Cavour had no idea how to bring up the photo on his computer. He hoped Montaro did.

Chapter Thirty-Three

That night, members of the Befanata troupe met in the piazza. Nick and Leah stood shoulder to shoulder, shivering in the damp cold, listening to the others chatter in excited anticipation of the cenone, the traditional meal the troupe would make from the food they had collected on their rounds of the Befanata.

Silvio and Giovanna were holding hands, as if nothing had happened between them at the Antoninis, and Angelina stuck to Italo's side like a cocklebur, cooing into his neck, snickering.

They all stood chatting at the corner outside the bar, waiting for Stefania and her friend. Silvio tapped his cigarette to shake off the ashes. Leah watched the smoke twist upward in the air.

As soon as Stefania and Primo arrived, they all set off into the old city, walking in ragged lines of twos and threes down the dark, narrow streets, where cats hunkered on the top steps of raised doorways and the bedclothes and pillowcases of preoccupied housewives, forgotten on the line, flapped in the damp night air above them.

Near the butcher shop, they turned down a small side street and from there into another narrow way, not more than a slot in the walls. Leah was reminded of the dromos.

Andrea stopped in front of a wooden door. The others gathered behind him and watched as he dug a key from his pocket and pulled a flashlight out of the bag he was carrying.

Nick put his arm around Leah's shoulder, holding her tightly against him. "Exciting, huh?"

Unable to shake a sense of foreboding, Leah nodded.

They all filed through the doorway, down a wide, stone stairwell to Signora Seta's cantina. Straight through the room was an open passage. It led to a long terrace, which spanned the length of the cantina and hung over the gorge and river below town. To the side of the terrace were two fruit trees and a patch of flowers, just outside the doorway of a smaller adjoining apartment where Signora Seta kept some kitchen things and a few chairs.

A sharp right at the bottom of the stairwell led to a ramp that descended into the cantina itself. Leah could make out the outline of barrels of wine hunkered on hewn stone platforms. A cave-like room with a rounded stone ceiling, the cantina had been dug out of the tufa centuries before, below what was now a three-story house. Tucked deep into the tufa, it maintained a perfect temperature for storing wine of 12 degrees Centigrade.

Straight through, past the ramp that led to the cantina, was a large, high-ceilinged room, curved at the top. The graceful, sweeping motions of the workmen who had hewn the stone were evident in the half-curve cut marks, as if they had been painted there from an artist's brush, rising and falling, one after the other, like waves of water.

"So what about Signora Seta?" Italo asked Andrea.

"Nobody's seen her."

Nick interjected. "I heard she went to the coast to meet a friend of hers from Rome, but nobody knows where she's staying."

Italo snorted. "Sounds like she had everything planned in advance. Maybe she's the one who did away with Giulio."

"Don't be stupid." Andrea glared at Italo. "They've called all over to find her. And when they do, it will be a terrible shock to her. Now let's do this!" He dangled the key in the air.

Giovanna had heard Italo. "Idiot! Don't talk that way, and stop intimating murder. Giulio fell. He tripped or something. That's all there is to it, and now he's gone." Her voice quivered.

Italo leered at her. "Boo-hoo. Now he's gone, and so is your source of drugs."

"Bastard! You're not even from here. You're nothing but a salesman who wants to pretend he's some sort of Tiburzi, while he sells appliances to people who can't afford them."

Hovering next to Italo, Angelina's face turned bright red and she raised her fist to strike.

Silvio caught her wrist midair. "Okay, okay. Giovanna, back off, and Angelina…"

"What?" She spat the word, staring intently at Silvio, twisting her arm, but unable to free herself from Silvio's grip.

"Giovanna didn't mean it. We're all on edge because of Giulio. Come on. Let's have the cenone and remember Giulio would have loved this; he would have wanted us singing, telling stories, drinking wine…. Okay?"

Angelina nodded; Silvio dropped her wrist.

Passing through the doorway to the large room Silvio whispered to Giovanna, "What's wrong with *her* tonight?

Giovanna sniggered. "Probably her dad."

Andrea called them to follow him back up the stairs, where they turned into another short flight of steps that led to a wide, low-ceilinged room with a stove in one corner, a table next to it, and a stack of chairs along the opposite wall.

Leah and the others each took a chair and started down again to arrange the table for the cenone.

The air seemed to have taken on a still chill Leah hadn't felt coming off the street. For a moment, she thought again of the burial cave where she had hidden from the killer. She shuddered, took a deep breath, and reminded herself where she was, that she was surrounded by friends.

Traipsing awkwardly downward, each one wrestling with a chair, they came to the lower landing, shuffled to the right, and wrangled the straight-backed chairs through a broad archway into the larger room. Leah set her chair on the rough tufa floor and glanced up to see narrow passageways, no larger than the spine of a fairly large book, situated high up in the walls.

Curious about several aspects of Signora Seta's rooms and cantina, she stepped out to take a closer look at the darkened cavern down the ramp.

"That's the cantina itself." Primo, a tall, thin man who had been in the

116

Befanata group, saw her peering into the darkness below the ramp. "I've got a flashlight if you'd like to go down."

"I would, thanks."

They descended the gentle slope of the ramp. Primo's penlight cast a dull glow a few feet ahead, faintly illuminating large barrels of wine arranged in lines along both walls.

"A perfect 12 degrees," he explained.

Leah already knew this, but she listened carefully, tilting her head to his darkened form. Primo spoke with gentle authority. "The constant temperature means these cantinas, here on the north side of town, are very valuable to people who make and sell wine, or even if they want to make wine only for themselves. It's rare these cantinas are up for sale. A wine dealer would kill to have one like this."

"Kill?"

"Sorry, an unfortunate slip. Just an expression. I mean a cantina like this is valuable, and Signora Seta is lucky to have it. Besides the financial aspects, it's a beautiful room in its way, no? Look at the walls, so perfect, so evenly chipped." He turned his penlight to the wall so Leah could see details.

"I noticed earlier. The skill of the workmen shows."

"You have a good eye if you noticed." Primo smiled, gratified she understood the aesthetic. "Do you have good taste as well, Signora? Perhaps you'll tell me which of the local wines you like the most?"

Leah laughed. Locals were always asking her which local wines she liked best and how the local wines compared to those of Piedmont or the Veneto.

"Don't try to trick me, Primo. I'm a visitor and I won't willingly offend anyone by naming the wrong wine."

He laughed. "Polite...*and* politic. Very good."

"Not so politic as you might think. I'm not a connoisseur. I seem to like whatever I'm given."

"Do you mean all Italian wines, or only the Scansansianese wines?"

Leah shook her head. "Only the local. I only drink local wines."

He joined in her laughter. "I can't trick you. You are resolutely diplomatic. And you are correct to drink local wines. We have the best—and it is difficult to choose among them."

"I'm doing my best to try them all."

In the dim light, she missed his warm smile.

"On another matter…" They were moving up the ramp toward the cenone gathering. "Nick mentioned to me that Italo has been telling him about the vie cave and Tiburzi. I hope Nick won't listen to everything Italo says. He's not an expert, and he dramatizes. The vie cave were not mysterious deep pathways carved out by the Etruscans.

"They weren't!" Leah was thinking of her article.

"Not exactly. It's a matter of time. They were Etruscan trails, but I don't believe they were originally carved as deep as they are now. I think it happened over time, with wear and repair."

"I've read that theory, but what about the burial caves along the sides?"

Just as Primo started to explain his own theory, which Leah knew was disputed, she was distracted by a hole about the size of a bushel basket at the edge of the ramp.

"What's that for?"

"Take a look."

Leah bent down and peered into the hole. In the dim light, she detected a huge, rounded cavern below. A waft of cool air made her jerk backward. She clapped her cupped hand over her nose and mouth. "Ehhhg! It smells rotten, like corpse flower."

"Can't be. Corpse flower doesn't grow here. Some people say this kind of hole was for burials, but it wasn't. It was just for bits of stone, pieces of wood and such."

He kneeled beside Leah and bent closely. "Ich! My God! That's disgusting. Move over a little and I'll reach my light down."

Primo drew a handkerchief from his pocket, covered his face, and leaned into the hole.

"The light's not bright enough to see the whole thing, but it's pretty empty I think. The smell might be from another apartment or room. Did you see those narrow airways high up on the wall in the other room?"

"Yes."

"They're like airholes, found in some of these refuse holes as well, and sometimes they connect with adjacent rooms, so maybe someone in this same building left something to rot in one of their dump holes, or in an adjoining cantina or apartment. I don't know. They're not supposed to do that." He brushed his hand through the air. "Let's get away from it and bring down the rest of the chairs."

Chapter Thirty-Four

Maneuvering the turns, Silvio and Andrea finessed a long folding table down the steps and set it in the middle of the large room. Stefania shuffled the chairs into place around it.

"Sit, everybody. The omelettes and sausages are almost ready."

She disappeared through the archway and up the stairs to the makeshift kitchen. Primo opened the homemade wine given them from the farmhouses they'd visited and poured for everyone. Andrea hefted his accordion onto his lap, slipped his arms through the straps, and sounded the first notes of one of the songs from the Befanata.

"May I?" Leah indicated a seat beside Italo and Angelina.

Italo drew back the chair. Leah smiled, but noticed Angelina was scowling. She remembered the conversation with Nick.

Leah, you've got to remember that foreigners always possess a certain exoticism, a certain attraction. You've interviewed enough people to know foreigners can be misunderstood. especially around women when you're interviewing men. You can't be your usual impetuous and friendly, open self. Somebody's bound to take it wrong.

Italo stood behind the chair waiting. "Well, are you going to sit?"

"Thanks, Italo. I'll sit beside Angelina, closer to the music. I like it loud, earsplitting."

Angelina made no acknowledgment when Leah sat beside her.

"Tell me about your work, Angelina. Someone said you're studying real estate."

Angelina grunted and leaned close to Leah in a mean hiss. "I know you're after Italo!"

"What?!" Leah jerked back.

"I saw the way you look at him." Angelina's face twisted. "And you'd better learn not to flirt with him. He's mine!" She tapped her chest with her index finger.

"I don't even know Italo!"

"That's not what I heard!"

"What could you have heard?"

"You were dancing close with him at the Antoninis."

In any other situation, Leah would have laughed, but Angelina had made her angry. "Well, you got it wrong."

"I doubt it. And don't try to pretend you've never seen me before." Angelina leaned into Leah's face.

Leah pushed her away. "I don't know if I have or not, maybe from a distance..."

"When was it?"

"I don't know." Exasperated, Leah had raised her voice. The others turned toward her.

Leah whispered, "Look. Let's start over. Let's not argue and spoil the evening. I promise you I have no interest in Italo, and I really would like to know about your work."

"Are you thinking of an article on my very interesting life?" Her grin thick with sarcasm.

"Just polite conversation, Angelina. That's all."

"Polite conversation." She flapped both hands in the air, "Well then. I'm a real estate agent—or will be. Not as exotic as being a writer from America who can afford to travel all the time."

"We all do different things."

"I'm sure," Angelina muttered through clenched teeth. Her breath was foul.

"Look, there's no reason to be sarcastic; if you don't want to talk, we don't have to, but there's no reason to create bad feelings, especially tonight."

"Shall we think of something neutral, then? Maybe child abuse. Maybe you'd like to talk about that." She tilted her chin in challenge.

"I…I..ah…"

"You don't seem eager for that topic."

"Angelina…"

"Cat got your tongue?"

"No, I just didn't expect such a combative conversation."

"Poor baby! Life can be so disappointing!" She made a face. "I don't care about child abuse and I don't care about you. Just stay away from Italo."

Leah experienced a confusion of emotions toward her. The insistent, childlike denial opened a slight crack in Angelina's tough, sarcastic exterior and showed what a wounded woman she was.

"You seem so cold, and yet you're obviously a tender woman. The way you love Italo."

"Tender! That's a laugh. I just don't want him to be taken away. And now I'd like to listen to the music if you don't mind."

Leah sighed and pushed her chair a little backward.

Chapter Thirty-Five

Andrea finished one song and started the next, and they all joined in, singing the songs they had sung in the farmhouses at the Befanata. When they struck up a waltz, Italo stood, took Angelina's hand, and led her away from the table to dance. Her movements, in contrast to Italo's grace, were stiff as sticks. She shifted from step to step, the upper part of her torso rigid, thick as a stone column. She pressed closely to Italo.

After the dance, Andrea, under the influence of four quick glasses of wine, called for Leah and Nick to sing an American song. When they both shook their heads in hopes he would pass them by, he began pounding the table.

"An A-mer-i-can song! And A-mer-i-can song! Put your c-mer-as away, and sing A-mer-i-can song!"

The others joined in and soon were all chanting and pounding the table in unison.

Nick whispered to Leah, "We have to do it. How about one of the Child Ballads?"

"Nick, no!" Leah pleaded. "The only Child Ballads I know are about murders. Actually, the only one I really know is 'The Willow Tree.'"

"Oh, not good." He thought for a minute trying to concentrate against the shouting and pounding.

"Look, they're not going to know the English, except maybe a few words."

Leah clenched her teeth. "It's still about a murder!"

"Come on! We have to do this; everyone's been generous with us, and it's a small thing."

"But nothing about a push off a cliff! I can't think!"

"Come on, it'll be okay."

"No! It won't... Wait, I've got it! 'How Many Miles to Babylon.'"

"Okay. It'll do." Nick turned to Andrea and reverted to Italian. "Okay, here goes."

He faced Leah. "On the count of three..."

How many miles to Babylon?
Three score miles and ten.
Can I get there by candle-light?
There, and back again ...

They sang off-key, hesitantly, in a somber, pale monotone, which blanched even more against the echoes of the naturally vivacious songs of the Befanata.

When they finished, the others clapped politely and nodded in good-willed sympathy.

Andrea spoke up. "Don't feel bad, you two. Not everyone can be musically inclined."

Andrea smiled and held out his hand to Nick, "We all needed a distraction, and you two were it. I don't think I've ever heard anything so bad."

Everyone at the table clapped and laughed.

Giovanna stepped through the doorway, carrying a large platter. "Let's eat and then we can sing again."

"Once our ears have had a good rest," someone quipped.

The platter was piled high with crisp sausages and huge round omelettes. Primo poured another round of wine, and they all dug in, cheered by the food, the singing, the friendly teasing.

When the platter was empty, Stefania lugged an enormous shopping bag from near the doorway, put it on the table, and pulled out cakes and biscotti, all gifts from the houses they had visited.

"Wait!" Andrea spread his hands to stop everyone from reaching for the sweets. "Signora Seta wanted us to have some of her famous Luisa Seta fragolino wine from two years ago. Remember how sweet and smooth it was?" He pulled a long key from his pocket and waved it in the air. "It's in the little apartment. I'll get it."

Italo jumped up, upsetting a glass of wine that flowed in a red sea across the table. "Sorry! But do you want me to get it, Andrea, while you go ahead and play?"

Angelina slipped her arm through Italo's, pulling him back into his chair. "You're not a servant. Let him go," she smirked, tilting her head toward the others. "They should be waiting on you, not you on them."

"I have to do it." His voice was adamant. "The rest of you stay here. I promised the Signora I wouldn't give the key to anyone else." He turned to Primo. "Can I use your flashlight?"

Primo frowned. "It's just a penlite. And not very good. Does anyone have a good flashlight?"

"Here's one," Stefania shouted. "Where is the Signora anyway; doesn't she know about…doesn't she know yet?"

"I heard she's gone to visit a friend, but they don't know where and can't contact her."

Andrea took the flashlight from Silvio and stepped under the archway to the terrace door. Outside, he turned to the other, smaller door, fit the key smoothly into the lock.

"I'm right behind you, Andrea."

Andrea erupted. "Leah, why did you come. I told you I preferred to get it myself. My aunt…"

They stepped into the apartment. A foul smell sent them reeling backward. Andrea pulled his shirt front over his nose, and Leah cupped her hand and scarf over her face. Near the narrow ramp that led downward into the second small, kitchen cantina, he tripped on a footstool. The flashlight tumbled out of his hand into the refuse hole by the side of the ramp.

"Shit!" he muttered, sucking air through his shirt as he dropped to his knees and crawled carefully toward the hole now illuminated by the light lying in the depths.

Andrea peered into the refuse pit, turned aside, and vomited.

Chapter Thirty-Six

"Andrea! What is it?"

He pointed, and Leah knelt beside him to peer into the hole. "Oh, dio! It's got to be Signora Seta!"

"I can't see the face."

"We've got to find out. Do you have rope?"

"You're not going down there?"

"I've got to. Maybe she's still alive. Call the Lieutenant and then get a rope."

Andrea's face had gone white. He stared into the hole.

Leah slapped him. "There's no time, Andrea. Call the Lieutenant and bring me a rope."

Andrea stood and pushed at the spot of vomit with his foot.

"Leave it!" Leah commanded. "Rope!"

Leah tied the rope to the leg of the heavy stove and lowered herself into the pit, where she dropped to her knees beside the body and put her hands gently on the woman's neck. She was dead. Leah lifted the hair from her face. It was Signora Seta.

"It is your aunt, Andrea. Pull me up."

"I'm not strong enough."

"Go get Nick and the others."

Chapter Thirty-Seven

"Get back! Nobody within three meters of the doorway!" Lieutenant Cavour yelled through the glove clamped over his mouth. He felt grief-stricken, angry at everyone. Signora Seta was a generous, good woman. He did not like being awakened at night for yet another body, did not like it that the body was in a pit, did not like that he could barely keep from vomiting. Neither did he like it that she may have given the best leads in Giulio's case. The relationship of the two dead was a clue in itself. But what? The cantina? The photos? Something else?

The Lieutenant was accustomed to dead bodies, but they were usually animal bodies, hog slaughter in the fall, a fallen cow in the fields. In Sardinia, he and Bibiana had helped neighbors on their farms. He knew death was not the opposite of life, but was a part of it, a part that took place in the circle of sustenance.

But this! What was this? What did a person have to say to himself to kill someone? What could make a person so angry they could kill and leave the body to rot? Who, like Cain, takes a stance with fiendish bravado and then cowardly tries to hide himself, to go simpering through life with a mark on his head? What adjustment did a person have to make to convince himself murder was a good idea? And if murder, why not worse? Why not cannibalism? What relief could it be just to kill and walk away?

And he had to deal with it. He wouldn't be going home to help Bibiana. He would be here choking, retching, dealing with the voids of people's evil acts.

He turned on Leah. *"Accidenti a te! Basta! Smettila!* You can't keep interfering, you've compromised the scene and..."

"But I haven't, Lieutenant. I didn't move anything. I thought maybe she was still alive, and it was important to find out as fast as possible."

"*Mi fa impazzire!*"

"I don't mean to drive you crazy. I just thought…"

"Well, stop thinking. Stop being…just go away."

Leah stepped back to join the rest of the group who were now hovered in a tight circle outside the doorway where Signora Seta had been found. The others pelted Andrea with questions, but he stood at the edge of the terrace, staring out over the gorge, and ignored them. Nick took Leah's arm and pulled her to the corner.

"Leah…" His face was red with anger.

"Don't, Nick. Just don't. I thought she might still be alive."

Nick stifled a yell.

Italo moved toward Andrea. Angelina barged through and pulled Italo away. "Let him be. He doesn't want us around right now." She flung a hand out toward the others. "And they don't either."

"We have to stay. The Lieutenant will want to ask questions."

"What are you talking about? It's chaos here; there's no reason to stay. They've got all our names, and Cavour said they could question everyone tomorrow in the office."

"Okay, okay." Italo was glad to have Angelina take control. He needed time to think.

Inside, at the edge of the hole, the Lieutenant tied a rope under the arms of Sergeant Gianicollo, helped him tie a scarf over his face, and lowered him into the opening, to make an official identification of the Signora's body.

"Why not just bring her up, give her the dignity of being in the funeral home?" Someone asked.

"I have to wait for forensics, damn it! You know that." Cavour hissed and turned to glare at Leah, who had stepped back next to Nick.

The Lieutenant had known the Signora from the first day he was assigned to Scansansiano. The disgusting odor, the blood, and the distortion of the corpse's limbs reflected none of Signora Seta's lively living warmth. He felt this death could push him to the edge of what was bearable. Why wasn't he at home in Sardinia, helping Bibiana? Why didn't people like Leah use their minds? Why didn't forensics get there? How long would he be forced to breathe the sickening odor?

At the bottom of the hole, kneeling on a towel, Gianicollo gently brushed the Signora's hair aside, then turned away and vomited violently against the curved wall. Her eyes, still open and set in a face puffed from rot and pale as lard, peered into the void of the cavern.

"Pull me up," he shouted. "It's her! Now get me outa here."

The words out of his mouth, Gianicollo gagged repeatedly until a small stream of yellow bile was all that oozed from his lips. He wiped his shirt sleeve across his face and shouted again, "Get me outa here, now!"

They hauled him slowly upward and out. Pale and trembling, he dragged the rope behind him as he rushed to the doorway and terrace to gulp fresh air.

The Lieutenant ordered everyone to stay away and stepped out to the terrace where he put his hand on Gianicollo's shoulder.

"Her head is bashed in Lieutenant. Maybe from the fall. She was stabbed in the stomach, more than once I'd say, but I didn't remove any clothing. It's just that there are tears in her dress, from the knife I suppose; and her bowels went, there's…stuff all over the place. That's the smell."

"I'm sorry. Listen, pull yourself together. Take names, addresses, and contact numbers, and then go on home and clean up. And take an extra two hours in the morning. I can handle whoever gets there before you come."

"Yes sir," Gianicollo nodded.

The Lieutenant herded everyone else back into the room where the cenone had been held.

"As I think we all know, it is Signora Seta, and she's been murdered. We'll need to take statements from all of you, but not tonight. Tonight just give your names, addresses, and contact numbers to Sergeant Gianicollo and come in to my office tomorrow morning. No excuses. I don't want to chase you all over the countryside to get in touch. Be there tomorrow!"

"Are the phones all working now?"

"Yes." He looked around the group, making eye contact.

"What about Italo and Angelina? They've gone."

"I told them they could go. I got their information from Angelina, and I also got…" he looked at his list, "Primo's information. Italo and Angelina are driving back for the night, and Primo had to get home. Something about his mother. But they'll all be in tomorrow. My office, early! All of you!"

He paused looking directly and steadily at each in turn. "Eight a.m."

Chapter Thirty-Eight

After Leah and Nick helped clean the dishes and put the chairs away, they walked home through the silent streets. Leah held Nick's arm, and they leaned into each other, avoiding the anger of earlier.

"I'm beginning to wonder if there wasn't something to that little tiff between Andrea and Italo."

Nick stopped. "My brain's addled. What do you mean?"

"That first house you went to last night. You told me Italo said Andrea would be glad if Giulio were dead. If I understood you, it was because Signora Seta would have given Andrea the cantina and those old photos if Giulio decided on moving down south like he'd talked about."

There is something funny there, and it may be true about Andrea, but I can't accept it. We know him; it just doesn't seem possible."

"Don't say we know him. We walked into his life at a certain chapter, but that doesn't mean we know the whole story. He's passionate about his photography; maybe he wants the photos just to possess them, not for money. It's confusing. I heard Miss Redhead say she thought there was some woman in the South and that woman and Giulio were, as she put it, an *item*."

"How do you hear all this gossip?"

Leah tapped her nose. " I think Giulio has probably had several 'items.' Giovanna was one of them from what the Antoninis said. And who knows? Maybe there were others; maybe he was the kind to get around. If Giovanna were jealous enough, well...just remember the Child Ballad we were about to sing at the cenone. Love can turn to jealousy and hate. And with drugs involved...."

But do you really think Giovanna could have done it?"

"She's strong enough if it's unexpected. So maybe, but then why the Signora?

Nick stopped for a minute and stared into the darkness as if he might see an answer, then went on. Their footsteps echoed against the stones of the street and facades of the houses.

"It seems Giovanna's anger would be toward Giulio," Leah said, "but you're thinking there is some connection between Giovanna and the cantina, or the photos?"

"I don't know. Maybe she has no connection to the cantina, and she killed Giulio because he was seeing someone else."

"But that implies two killers."

"I don't know. I wonder about Silvio too, but I can't figure out his connection to the cantina or the photos, and there would have to be for the double murders to make sense."

"We pretty much have to assume that the same person killed both Giulio and Signora Seta, right?"

"It's logical. It would be too coincidental otherwise. How many murders do you think you'd find in a small Tuscan town? Unless maybe two people were working together.

"I didn't think of that." Leah pulled a tissue from her pocket and blew her nose.

"You'll wake the whole street!" Nick laughed.

"Be serious, Nick. Who knows who else could be involved? Nobody we know seems likely, but I'm beginning to think that except for the Antoninis, we don't really know anyone. It's thrown me. Maybe we like some people because we *don't* know them. Remember Ronnie? We *knew* him, and I was sure he was a friend, but as soon as he found out we didn't agree with a certain aspect of his politics, he dropped us. I know it's way less serious than murder, but the principle is the same."

"You're right, but you know it'll happen again, probably a few times. People will disappoint us, and we'll disappoint others. There are too many factors in anyone's life for it not to happen. So let's keep Ronnie tucked away and think about Italo. Italo's looking for a restaurant, doesn't seem interested in the photos, but is very interested in the cantina. Andrea is the reverse: interested in the photos, but not the cantina."

"They could have done an amicable exchange if Signora Seta willed them both to Andrea."

"But by all accounts, it would be willed to Giulio. Andrea was second in line. That fouls the amicable exchange and means Giulio has to go."

"Okay, but why kill the Signora? With Giulio dead, photos and cantina would have gone to Andrea. Problem solved."

"Unless Andrea needed money right away. Signora Seta was in good health from what I hear; she could have lasted a long time."

"He would have had to give her time anyway, to change the will. Killing her would be shooting himself in the foot."

"But he would be the next of kin, the only one left. I think the law reads that the heirs succeed jointly to the estate in both assets and liabilities in equal portions – unless the will says differently."

"Both dead, no wait, no sharing."

"And a smooth, amicable exchange with Italo."

"No. Andrea doesn't like him. He'd never sell to Italo. But it all could have been solved by convincing the Signora simply to split the property."

"She was in too good of health. Both Giulio and Andrea would have been waiting, probably for years. Maybe they were both in a hurry."

"Since Giulio's dead, it seems like it was Andrea."

"It seems evident, but I can't believe it. It doesn't feel right. And it seems like he wouldn't take a chance on his future."

"You're right. I really do think one of these days someone from National Geographic or one of the other big magazines will discover him, and he won't need to worry about money—but does *he* know that?" She turned to Nick, "If I get out of here alive, I'm going to buy one of his portraits."

Nick kissed the top of her head. "I'm going to make sure you get out of here alive, but for me to do that, you need to stay close and *not* go out alone."

Chapter Thirty-Nine

The next morning, just before first light, Leah slipped out of bed, carefully lifted her clothes from the back of the chair, and tiptoed into the living room. Nick turned on his side, groaned, and fell back into a deep sleep, breathing heavily, rhythmically.

Leah dressed quietly, took her jacket and a house key from off the hooks at the entryway, and stopped.

Something seemed strange. She put her hand to the door and slid it carefully along the opening until she felt the doorknob. There was a string attached to it. Moving her finger down the side of the string she came to a large cowbell.

She stifled a laugh. Nick's way of making sure he would hear if she tried to leave.

She took a knife from the pocket of her jeans and, holding the clangor of the bell, cut the string. She laid the bell carefully on the chair by the door, slowly turned the doorknob, pulled it to, and edged out, closing the door with a slight click.

Tucking her arms in the sleeves of her jacket, she scuttled through the damp air looking forward to a hot coffee before she descended into the gorge and the trail that would lead her to Via Cava San Raffaello. The narrow streets were quiet in the muted light of predawn, and she relished the chill of the morning air. At Via Vezzosa she glanced to the side toward the little piazzetta that hung over the gorge. Clouds were settled low; it was too beautiful a sight to pass up. She turned off the street on the narrow walkway that led to the piazzetta, where she could have the full view.

Secondo was not on his usual bench. She stepped forward and leaned over the wall. Below, a flock of sheep dotted a meadow by the river, and she could see the roof of what had been the old mill, where, Carla had told her, the women used to do their laundry and where the young people went to picnic on Sunday afternoons.

At a slight movement behind her, Leah spun around. On a bench in the shadow at the far side of the piazzetta someone was wrapped head to toe in blankets. Leah's heart pounded; it wasn't where Secondo slept. She moved away from the wall toward the street, but as she did, the man under the blankets poked out his head and croaked, "What are you doing here?"

It was Secondo.

"I'm sorry, Secondo. I didn't mean to wake you. I didn't see you; you're not on your usual bench. You're in shadow."

Secondo swiped away his long, oily mass of dark tangles. He was a handsome man with a high forehead, aquiline nose, and olive skin, stereotypically Italian. He had spent the night rough, was disheveled, and needed a good scrub, but Leah realized that at one time, if there had been a time for him, he must have broken hearts.

Still, her voice carried the tension she felt in her neck and back. Nick had told her Secondo was harmless, but she remembered the strange glee on his face when there was a fight outside the bar and how he had followed her. She eased toward the walkway that led to the street.

Secondo stared at her. Leah stopped. Something about his look.

She stood still, held in the grip of his steady gaze. He reminded her of another man, a farmer who lived near where she had grown up. When he was young, the man and his wife had run a small, but thriving farm. After his wife died, he neglected the farm. His small acreage lay fallow and his flocks of chickens dwindled to ten, just enough for a few eggs for himself and some to sell for a pittance to neighbors.

The man had withdrawn, living on the edge of their rural society, keeping to himself, wandering disheveled and dirty around town, in and out of the stores on rainy days. Friendly enough, he greeted people in his taciturn way, but as he walked away, there were those who tapped their heads with their index fingers and smiled. An act of petty cruelty, and by her silence, she had been part of it without giving it a thought.

She assuaged her sense of guilt by joining some of the community who watched over the man, leaving food and clothing on his doorstep, paying his heating in the winter.

Ironically, years later, after this shadow of her community had died and the sheriff had come to take his body, the officer found thousands of dollars in the cold mouth of the man's stove, under his mattress, and in the gallon-sized tin cans that he had stored at the back of his foul-smelling cupboards. For years, he had invested his money, living frugally, and letting his profits literally pile up. In his will, he left all the money to the little town library, with the simple statement: *For those of you who are cruel, you'll learn better; for those of you who are kind, you'll find even more ways to be kind; and most of all for you children, so through books, your eyes will see to the ends of the earth, to all wonders.*

These memories in mind, Leah faced Secondo. She felt wary and remembered her last encounter with him on the trail. Was he capable of murder? Wouldn't he have attacked her by now? Was he mentally unstable? A loose cannon?

Still, she had the sense of how cold it must have been for him all night on the bench. She reached into her pocket, retrieved the liras she had gotten in change from her groceries a few days before, and stepping forward, handed the money to Secondo. As she did, she wished she could have done it in a more gracious way, but wouldn't refrain because of circumstances. Looking him straight in the eyes, she said, "Bless you, Secondo, have some coffee and brioche. It will soon warm up a bit."

He stared at her for a few seconds, looked down at the money, looked back at her, then did something Leah hadn't expected. He bent over, carefully set the money on the pavement, stood, and reached his hand toward her.

She held out her own, taking his smooth palm, surprised by his firm grip. His voice was deep, mellow.

Thank you, Signora. I left my money at home and now I don't have to go back to get it before I have coffee. Don't worry about me. I like sleeping

136

outside, even when it's cold. It's less lonely in the company of the stars and the sky."

"Rest, Secondo."

"Okay."

"And please don't follow me, okay?"

"I never know what I'll do." He smiled.

Leah shook her head and, with a slight smile, turned to leave.

Sabina, the young woman who had the early shift at the bar, broke off her conversation with an old man sitting alone at a table in the corner.

She greeted Leah cheerfully. "Again this morning? The usual?"

"Please." Leah had mixed feelings about such blatant cheer first thing in the morning.

The old man grunted in frustration at the interruption. He downed his grappa and slammed the empty glass on the table, grumbling at Sabina to bring him another.

Sabina looked at Leah, hunched her shoulders, and stepped behind the counter to fetch the grappa.

Leah knew the man. It was Leo, a recently retired postal worker, who had been woefully ill-suited to the work. It would have been better if he had been a farmer or shepherd, work where he could have been alone most of the time, with visits to the bar when he came to town for supplies and a chat with the young women. At the post office, where Leah had had her own encounter with him on one of his particularly nasty days, he hated greeting the endless string of people with their picky complaints about bills and packages, each one joggling for a place line. And this morning, he hated being interrupted in his conversation with the luscious young barmaid.

He turned toward Leah with a menacing look. "You'd be better off staying away from those damn vie cave. You never know who could be up there."

"I've got to finish an article. But…" she paused, "who do you think could be up there? Do you know of someone?"

"What are you? The town detective?" He huffed, and muttered, "God damn stupid women."

Sabina laughed, "Never mind, Leo, you can't push our buttons. We won't respond to your nastiness." She winked at Leah.

Leah stood. "Thanks. A great cappuccino as always."

"Be safe."

Leah picked up her jacket, wondering how she could be safe when she knew she was setting out impetuously. She had pushed the article to the back of her mind, hoping she could find some sort of clue on the trail, on table rock, or in the burial cave. She felt instinctively something must have been dropped, some tiny bit of evidence the police had overlooked.

Just as she stepped out the door, another customer, head tilted against the morning breeze and securing a broad-brimmed hat with one hand, bumped into her.

"Sorry!" Leah skittered aside, apologizing.

No response but a grunt. Leah hurried on her way.

Chapter Forty

On the far side of the field across from the opening of the via cava, sheep were grazing in the wet grass. One lamb butted against its mother's teats, ready to feed. The ewe placidly continued to graze, as if oblivious to the minor battle under her belly. The scene reminded Leah of Sara as a baby, greedily nursing.

"Ahhhh!" She exclaimed, remembering Sara would be coming soon, perhaps too soon.

Leah shook her head. This was the story of her life. Hurried, distracted, compelled to move one hundred miles an hour in a dozen different directions. She sighed and passed under the glassed-in figure of San Raffaello embedded in the rock overhang at the entrance to the trail. Within a few steps, she was enshrouded in the dusky light between the towering walls.

Ascending, she passed through the deep, narrow slits of rock to intermittent open spaces, where the stone of the via cava glistened in the morning light. In these small plots of earth where the rock walls opened to forests and small meadows, there was a sheen of dew across the delicate grasses and weeds, and Leah could look out over the gorge. Languid clouds glided upward through the trees, slowly dissipating as the sun crept over the eastern horizon.

In spots where the sun couldn't reach, the walls of the pathways were covered with a thick, brilliant green moss, soft, moist to the touch. Along the undercuts at the bottom of the walls, water seeped through deep cracks and dripped into the narrow slit of a side channel that directed rain and run-off through openings in the walls toward the scattered bits of flat, treeless spaces that dotted the thick forests. Rivulets of rainwater tumbled gently from hollow to hollow and wet Leah's shoes. Taking a quick step up a broken spot in the trail, she slipped on moss and threw her hand against the rock wall just in time to prevent herself from falling. The scabrous rock abraded her hand and she pulled it to her, flexing the fingers in and out to dispel the stiffness.

Righting herself, she thought she heard a faint laugh. She stood still and listened. Only the early morning breeze in the leaves.

This walk was different for Leah than that of two days earlier. That someone had made her run away, chased her, and wanted to kill her insulted her. It was a travesty, a perversion visited on the life of the now dead, on the shocked and aggrieved community. The murders and the attempt on her life made her furious at a profound, visceral level. No matter what Nick or the Lieutenant said, Leah was not interested in cowering in her apartment while the men did the work of finding the killer. Leah wanted justice, and that meant *doing* something.

Glad for the thick grip of her running shoes, Leah moved upward at a rhythmic pace, brushing the sides of the walls with her hands for the pleasure of feeling the rough, wet texture of the tufa.

Ahead, at a bend in the trail, a clump of flowering cyclamen had burst from a crack in the sheer wall; these were the flowers she had seen the day of the murder. She stopped to bend down and put her face to deep crimson blossoms. Thick, velvety, they were not as large as commercial cyclamen, but were more real, more beautiful in their sturdy wild form. She thought for a moment of picking them to take back to Nick, but checked herself. She had a long way to go, and they would be wilted by the time she got home.

And besides, why would I want to kill one of the most beautiful things I've seen today?

She hurried on toward the table rock.

Chapter Forty-One

Nick woke with a start. The workmen who were refurbishing the house up the hill were hammering. Nick yelled "Damn it! Can't a person get any sleep?" He checked the clock on the nightstand and turned toward Leah. She wasn't there.

"Lea…ah!" he called to the outer room. "Bang on the ceiling, would you? Maybe those guys will stop." As soon as he said it, he realized the workmen were further up the hill and would not hear her.

"Leah?"

No response.

Déjà vu.

"It didn't work."

He grabbed at his clothes and stumbled into the outer room for his shoes, a sweaty fear trickling down his back.

Chapter Forty-Two

On a high ledge above the trail a figure dressed in dark clothes, face obscured by a turtle-neck sweater and hat, crouched in the vines at the lip of the sheer wall, looking down on table rock, rifle in hand.

Below, Leah quickened her pace. She was breathing heavily and panted with relief when she stepped onto table rock. She sat, rested a moment, then rose and began a search of each nook and cranny of the ledges and stone seat.

When, in a crack at the edge of the seat, a glint of silver caught her eye, she got down on her knees and fingered a heavy silver and leather bracelet with frayed eye and knot fastener from the little crevice. The bracelet was crudely worked and well worn.

Leah's heart was pounding. *I knew there'd be something. I knew it!*

Excited, she headed down trail, toward town.

The sound of a loud crack was simultaneous with a sensation of sudden wind near her cheek. Leah jerked her arms upward to cover her head from falling rock.

A second bullet took her in the left arm. It snapped her humerus and opened a hole in the underflesh, three inches above the elbow. Leah dropped onto the trail. There was no pain. Gazing upward, she saw the walls of the via cava lean inward, as if they were closing over her, yet simultaneously drifting away. She noted a black shape floating through the brush. The sky appeared infinitely far above her, the stark blue of first light, darkening. *A storm?* She felt a sensation of what, rain? under her arm, and turned her head to see blood seeping through her jacket onto the rocks.

"Cut myself," she muttered just before she blacked out.

A figure approached, looked down, and reached for the bracelet still clutched in Leah's hand. Blood darkened the rock at Leah's side. The figure turned to the ascending trail and hurried upward toward the road on the ridge, laughing.

Chapter Forty-Three

Secondo pulled the blanket from around his shoulders and neck and tossed it to the ground. Walking at a good pace had given him warmth, although in the shadow of the via cava it was damp and chill. Cold from the long night on the bench had seeped through his blanket and the three layers of summer clothes he had scavenged from the town dump, but moving he felt fine.

He advanced at a quick pace. His ragged clothing disguised a muscular frame, which he had built from constant wandering up and down the gorges, along the vie cave, through the streets of the town. He had not eaten since late morning the day before, and the caffeine and carbohydrates of the coffee and brioche coursed straight through his system, leaving him energized, at least for an hour or two. He felt good.

For some years after the first manic incident in his early twenties, Secondo resisted the truth of the illness. He rarely slept, and he cajoled as many women as he could into his bed. His friends encouraged him and laughed at his antics, living vicariously through his wild ways, envying his boundless energy. Secondo raced through the days, laughing with them, oblivious to the trail of sadness in his wake. His spending sprees continued long enough to ruin him and his mother, who wore the permanent make-up of grief.

His manic flights continued until late one autumn afternoon on the via cava. Secondo had scaled a steep slope ten meters to the top, and standing on top was certain he could leap the width of the trail below into the brush on the other side.

He spent two months in hospital.

"An accident," his mother explained to the doctor. "An accident."

She coaxed Secondo, who had gone from mania to depression, into taking the medications. A doctor from Siena provided antipsychotics and a mood stabilizer.

It was the beginning of what seemed to Secondo an endless round of experimentation with drugs. He was willing to take them, but no combination worked. They made him nauseous, he felt drugged. He gained weight; he lost weight. He was no longer manic, but had trouble sleeping or he slept too much. He lived in a haze. His friends drifted away. He missed the ecstasies of mania. He didn't want to come down; he didn't want to be down.

Worse than any of it, he had ruined their life financially. He could now see it, and every day he lived with the shame of his recalcitrance, his deadly energy, that foolish jump.

Secondo had grown up in the town and in the forests that sheltered the vie cave. Seeing he struggled to be healthy, to be a part of the community, some townspeople in turn helped him as they were able. These people were the ones who retained in their spirits the understanding that children can heal the soul, and being perceptive of Secondo's childlike mental state compounded with bipolar illness, gave whatever quiet support they could to his mother and him.

His mother forgave him the daily drama, doling out the pills when the stream of his blood reversed in his veins, and the hypomania—or worse, mania itself—compelled him again to frenetic days, sleepless nights, and wild behavior. The illness dogged him relentlessly, turning the world gray in depression, and then bright in a mania that spun him like a leaf in an autumn wind. His mother followed. Where he went, she went, to care for him, perhaps the only one in the community who knew that underneath the illness there was an intelligent, capable man struggling alone to climb an impossibly high wall.

His mother refused to subject him to the embarrassment of seeing a psychiatrist; because she knew the ingrained fear and shame some in the community felt toward mental illness. It was only by the weight of her grief and the clear power of her love, evident in every word, that she was able to convince a Roman doctor to arrange the medication by phone, with only yearly visits. She guarded the medication, secreting it away in the small apartment.

Thus, in the years before his mother's death, still under her care, Secondo improved, and he relied on her to keep him balanced, well.

It couldn't continue. Days before she died, his mother went to her friend Marcella and told her she had arranged for Secondo's medication to be sent to her house. Marcella promised to guard it and to take Secondo to Rome for his yearly check-up.

Secondo's mother went home. She told Secondo he would soon be getting his medicine from Marcella.

"Do as I ask, Secondo. You are much better now. It's the medicine, and Marcella will make sure you get it, but she can't force you. You'll have to do that on your own. I won't be here to help you."

When he heard this, Secondo jerked toward her. "Why?"

His mother ignored his question. "I've made a calendar to remind you, and Marcella will refill your pill box when it's needed. Do it for me, Secondo, and for yourself. Marcella won't talk about it to anyone."

She died an uneasy death a few days after this conversation, and Secondo was alone in the apartment.

Walking upward along the trail, Secondo remembered his mother's words. He had honored them and wished he could tell her. After years of resisting, he watched the calendar every day, took the medicine, and though he tried to banish the hope from his mind, he felt capable, felt as if he could work, could have a real job.

So, he allowed himself to dream of being a street sweeper. He imagined himself with the long broom handle in his hands, the twigs of the broom curved from the sweeping motion: back and forth, back and forth along Via Vezzosa.

His daydream was broken by the report of a rifle.

Chapter Forty-Four

The run up the hill and across the piazza to the police state winded Nick. He gulped air, straightened his jacket, and shook his hands loose at his sides, taking in a few more deep breaths to calm himself before he entered. Signorina MacCleod was sure to notice if he were disheveled or out of breath, and within minutes the news would be broadcast from her desk telephone throughout town. Drawing in one last deep breath, he pressed the door handle and entered.

The Signorina, flaming red hair floating in a wide sweep around her head, looked up from the mystery she was reading, making no attempt to hide the book and the fact she was squandering the public's money on the time she spent reading detective stories with lurid covers. Spurred on by the exciting thought of dark handsome detectives and bodacious blonds professing love in the midst of gunfire, her greetings were particularly perky.

"Signor Contarini! You're up early this morning."

"Yes, is the Lieutenant in?"

"Don't you even want to say hello?"

"Of course, but…"

"He's here for a few minutes. Giulio's death, and now Signora Seta…you can imagine…"

She stared at him as if she expected him to say something about the deaths. He wondered how much she really knew.

"I'm sure he's very busy, but I need to speak to him now." He hadn't meant to be emphatic.

She made a face. "Such a rush!"

She approached the Lieutenant's door with her usual languid swing of the hips, a slow pendulum under her tight gray skirt. Her high-heeled boots clicked with each step, pounding in Nick's head.

She opened the door. "The American is here, Lieutenant."

Nick heard a muted response, and the Signorina turned to Nick, knitted her eyebrows, and motioned him in. He brushed by her, waiting until she returned to her desk, then closed the door with a swift snap behind him.

"She what?!"

"She's gone back to the via cava."

"Stupid woman!" The Lieutenant's anger turned his olive skin to a deep red.

"At the moment, I agree with you Lieutenant, and that's why I came to you rather than simply going after her myself. If we both go this time, and you give her another stern warning, maybe it will do some good. Can't you jail her or something?"

"You want me to put your wife in jail? For what? Being bullheaded, mulish, obstinate, impetuous, foolhardy, reckless…I can't jail her for her personality. God knows how you stand it."

Cavour rubbed his forehead, his eyes closed. "Santa Madonna!" He looked at Nick who was silent, caught between wanting to defend Leah and agreeing with the Lieutenant.

"Your wife, Signor, is a great deal of trouble, and I have too much trouble already, but yes, I suppose I must go—with the hope this is the last time. I'm afraid your wife is rapidly becoming persona non grata," he paused, "no matter how much I like you two!"

Shocked by the idea they could be sent away, Nick tried to distract him. "Have you been able to bring up the picture yet? Can you see a face?"

The Lieutenant heard what Nick said, but let it pass as if he hadn't. Montaro had been working the photo for hours, but had been unsuccessful. The Lieutenant did not want to tell Nick that Montaro was in the next room, even then.

"There's nothing for it. We'll have to use valuable time to go looking for her." He gave Nick a hard stare. "Why can't you control her?"

"Have you been able to control the women in your life, Lieutenant?"

The Lieutenant gave a slight cough. "That's not the point!"

"You know it is the point, Lieutenant. Look, I'm assuming she went back toward table rock for possible clues. Let's just go."

In the police car, Cavour continued to vent his anger. "You must talk to her, convince her it's dangerous."

"I can only say what I said before, 'Can *you* convince *your* women of anything, once they've set their minds to it?'"

A vision of his sister slugging their uncle crossed the Lieutenant's mind. He smiled. "I suppose you are right. Women are difficult to deal with. All the same, you can see that I have no time to chase up and down the vie cave to corral your wife."

"But the vie cave are her business...the article."

"The article! The article! But not murder, not clues, not danger! I can't believe she's up there working on the article. You said it yourself just now! I want you both to stay put. You muddy the waters and steal our time when we need to be working."

"She did bring the photo...that should be the most help of all, when you can bring it up."

"Don't shift it on me, on our computers, and don't try to change the subject!"

There was a loud honk behind them. Cavour had taken the curve too fast and was forced to slam on the brakes, and then accelerate again as the car behind him closed in.

Nick took a deep breath, imagining he and the Lieutenant were the next likely to be killed, not by a bullet or a fall, but in a car accident. He wanted to change the subject from Leah. "Who would have known that there would be two murders in a small town like this?"

"What? Don't you live in a rural area in America? Do you think people in small towns don't suffer the same hatreds and angers like people in New York or Chicago? Do you think we're all just boring people with no passions?"

"I didn't say that! And you know I'm not from a big city. It just seems so calm and quiet here." Hands against the dashboard, Nick steadied himself.

"Ok. I know you didn't say it. You two have been good citizens, mostly... and I know you love it here. Like the rest of us. It's been decades since there's been a murder, well before my time." He shook his head from side to side. "I just can't figure out why anyone would want to kill Giulio or Signora Seta. It's this cantina business."

Chapter Forty-Five

Secondo stopped and stared. As if she had gently fallen backward, arms crooked shoulder high, Leah lay unconscious on the trail. Her blood seeped onto the stone, pooling in one of the depressions made over the centuries by the hooves of donkeys on their rounds to and from the fields above.

"*Madonna Mia!*" he whispered and ran forward to bend over her. With a delicate movement, he pulled at her sleeve, unable to tell if the blood was coming from her side or her arm. He feared most it was from the chest, the heart. The heart would not be good.

"What should I do?"

He stood and looked down the trail, then up the trail, then above to the top of the steep walls. There was no one to help.

A stream of sweat dripped into his eyes; he swiped his arm across his brow and shuffled his feet. "*Mio Dio! Mio Dio!*" He knelt again beside Leah.

"I saw it and I can do it."

Shaking his head back and forth he rose, unbuttoned his shirt, and searched for a stick. With the sharp end, he poked at the shirt until he made a tear large enough to put his fingers through, just below the neckline. Taking the shirt in both hands, he ripped a broad strip of material free from the shirt.

Tourniquet in hand, he strained to remember what his mother had said when he watched her once put a tourniquet on Marcella. Marcella had cut her upper arm to the bone on a sharp wire while she was climbing through the fence of her sheep pen near the river. Secondo and his mother, on their way to picnic in the shade along the water found her, and Secondo's mother had bound Marcella's arm, urging Secondo to watch as she did.

Now, he talked himself through it.

"Not too thin. If it's too thin, it will damage the tissue and be too tight."

"Put it between the cut and the heart."

"Now under the arm and on top a square knot."

"Now a stick through the loop of the knot."

"Now a twist and a twist, gentle, not tight."

Hands trembling, he gently eased the cloth under Leah's upper arm, tied a knot, slipped the stick through, and then twisted, until he saw the flow of blood diminish and stop. He checked to make sure the tourniquet was not too tight, and wrapped the loose ends of the cloth around the stick, tucking the ends gently into the strap around her arms so the tourniquet would hold.

Finished, Secondo stood and looked again up and down the trail, hoping help would appear. There was no one. He inhaled a deep breath, bent, and carefully scooped Leah into his arms.

"I'm doing this," he said to the air, grunting as he lifted her. "I'm doing this." He adjusted her on his lifted knee, stood, and stepping carefully, turned down the trail.

She was light, but before long he was dripping with sweat. The limp weight had grown heavier and heavier, and he was forced to stop every few paces to raise his knee and rebalance her on his thigh while he righted his grip under her arms and legs. Gravity and the descent worked against him; it took all Secondo's strength to hold her safely to his chest.

Reaching the spot where he had dropped his blanket, he laid Leah carefully in the middle of it, straightened the edges, and then wrapped the blanket around her. She was pale, cold, even if she couldn't feel it. Just like Marcella.

Secondo stretched his arms and back, then bent to lift Leah once again and continue down the via cava, heel first against stone, then rolling carefully forward. So intent was he on his footing that when he rounded the last turn before the via cava opened into the field, he failed to see Lieutenant Cavour and Nick striding along the field's edge. It was only when Nick cried out, "What have you done!" that Secondo saw them.

He stopped abruptly. Nick, with the Lieutenant on his heels, was running toward him.

"Stop!" The Lieutenant yelled.

"I am stopped," Secondo yelled back.

Nick and the Lieutenant came beside him. Nick looked angry. The Lieutenant spoke to Secondo. "Yes, you are stopped."

His hands trembling, Nick carefully pulled back the blanket which had fallen over Leah's face. She was unconscious, her skin alabaster, cold to his touch. He leaned close to her mouth and could feel her breath burst in faint puffs against his cheek. He emitted a sudden loud gasp, tears pouring from his eyes.

"Thank God, thank God."

Secondo yielded her to Nick. "I put on a tourniquet. Somebody shot her in the arm."

Nick nodded. "You take her legs Secondo, I'll hold her shoulders. The Lieutenant will bring the car closer."

Secondo had been even-tempered for over two years now, but many people had heard the gossip and even the townspeople had imprisoned the memory of his past behavior in their minds and in that way refused to let him improve. They remained wary, perpetually unsure of his state of mind. He had come to accept it, but at this moment he experienced a convergence of great joy and desolate frustration. These men were trusting him, asking him to help. Set beside the reality of daily life as a man stigmatized, it was too much. Joy and pent-up anger were battling inside him. He couldn't move.

"Secondo!" The Lieutenant called back. "There's no time to lose. Let's get Leah in the car. You've done a great job."

"I know I did a good job! I *know* it!" His voice was thick with indignation.

"I'm sorry! Please. Let's get Leah to a doctor, and we can talk there."

The Lieutenant could not remember Secondo seeming that normal, and he flushed at how condescending he must have seemed to the man who, he hoped, had saved Leah's life.

Chapter Forty-Six

"I've got her now."

Nick shifted to slide his arm under Leah's legs and take her full weight on his own. He rested her against the back fender of the car. Secondo opened the door, and Nick turned sideways, bent, and stepped into the car holding Leah close. Secondo shut the door behind him.

Sitting quietly in the front seat, Secondo glanced in the rearview mirror to watch Nick cradling Leah.

"I found her!" Secondo blurted.

Nick looked in the mirror. "Yes, Secondo. You didn't only find her, you saved her life."

"Now she won't be afraid of me."

The Lieutenant spoke. "She'll always remember that you saved her life, Secondo, and all the people in town will remember it too."

Secondo smiled.

He fell silent and thought about Leah. Even afraid, she had been kind and generous. Her fears of him, he reasoned must be similar to his fears for himself. When would the illness strike? What would he do when it did? He had caused his mother much grief, had disappointed the women who loved and believed in him, lived in fear of wonderful sweet mania that felt so good and carried him so high, and dreaded the gray emptiness of depression when he couldn't feel, couldn't move from the couch. Finally, he had ruined his mother's life, the life of the only woman who had stayed with, fought for, and loved him until she died.

I've never hurt anyone physically; they know that I did steal the money from

154

Signora Carlotta, but even when she caught me and beat me with a broomstick, I didn't fight back. I threatened her, but I didn't do anything, and I gave the money back, and I didn't hurt her. I hope Leah doesn't know. I saved her today. But maybe that's not enough. Maybe there's too much gossip, so many people know so much about me... Maybe I will never be enough.

He looked in the rearview mirror again. Leah's head hung over Nick's forearm.

"Secondo, after the hospital you need to come to the station to make a statement." The Lieutenant was taking the curve fast. In the rearview mirror, Secondo saw Nick lean under the weight of Leah in his arms.

"Take it easy," Nick hissed, "I can barely hold her.

"Of course I'll make a statement. That's what witnesses do."

Chapter Forty-Seven

J ust as they reached the top of the hill toward the new part of town and the hospital, the two-way radio emitted a burst of static and a voice stuttered, "Montaro to Lieutenant. Come in, Lieutenant."

The Lieutenant reached to lift the speaker from its hook and flipped a switch on the side. "Montaro! I can't talk now!"

The rotund, bald-headed computer specialist sitting in front of the radio in the station, grasped the transmitter tightly in his beefy fingers and laughed nervously.

"But Lieutenant, you said the photo was important, and you wanted to know as soon as I could bring it up. I have. It's been a real bear to work with, something about the interface…"

"Okay, okay. I don't need the whole story. I'm on my way to the hospital."

"Hospital!"

"Never mind. I'll tell you later. Just give me the essentials."

"Ok. I've got the photo, but am having trouble enlarging it. It should be easy. I can't figure out why—"

"Essentials, Montaro!!"

"There's just what looks like the two men. The killer has his back to the camera, sort of. You can see a little of the outline of the face. The hat covers the hair and makes a shadow, but things will be clearer if we enlarge it. There's a kind of glint."

"Well, keep working, damn it! And don't bother me again unless you know who it is!"

Montara exhaled heavily, glad to ring off. Cavour slammed the little radio back on its hook.

From the back, Nick whispered, "I thought you were familiar with the computer."

Cavour squirmed in his seat. "For the basic things, and this should have been basic. Don't worry, Montaro will get it figured out.

"It damn well better be soon." He looked down at Leah.

The hospital, a large, rectangular structure three stories high with windows spaced like soldiers along the length of it, stood on a hill on the far side of town, one of the last buildings before the countryside. At one time the outer walls had been painted a bright white with blue trim that sparkled in the sunshine. That was before the war, and when the Lieutenant pulled carefully into the emergency lane, Nick noticed in the way one sees detail in sharp relief during trauma, that the paint was chipped and the trim faded to a dull gray.

Easing to a stop, Cavour flung the driver's door wide and ran ahead while Nick struggled to lift Leah out of the back seat without bumping her inert body against the sides of the door. Secondo waited, his hands outstretched.

"It's okay, Secondo. I've got her. You go ahead and get the door."

Nick hunched his shoulder to wipe the drops of sweat from his ears and with his last strength, carried Leah sideways through the door into the hospital. Cavour had alerted the emergency room. A nurse was waiting with a gurney, and Nick laid Leah down gently.

Blood seeped onto the sheets of the gurney. Nick sucked air; his heart was pounding. Sweat mingled with the tears streaming down his cheeks, and he reached for the edge of the sheet to wipe his face.

The nurse clipped away the makeshift tourniquet and bandage. "Don't worry, Signor. She has a serious wound, but not a fatal one, although it could have been. You did a very good job on the tourniquet. Otherwise, she wouldn't be here."

"It wasn't me."

Secondo had stepped through the curtained area just in time to hear the nurse. "I saw my mother do it once. And I saw it again on one of those doctor shows on American TV."

"Secondo?" the nurse exclaimed. "It was you?"

"Yes."

"Well, you can be proud of it. And it's good to hear of a good thing from America. I thought it was all gangsters and murderers over there. Still, I imagine your mother was a better teacher."

Secondo shook his head. "She was, but America's okay. The nature shows are good too."

Chapter Forty-Eight

L eah opened her eyes a few minutes before noon the next day. Without moving her body, she slowly turned her head side to side, trying to figure out where she was. Plain white walls. Stretching a little more to the side, she dropped back with a yelp of pain and stuck out her tongue to wet her lips. Her mouth was painfully dry. Her left arm ached. There was a tube coming from the vein in the crook of her elbow. Following the trail of the tube to a stand, she noted two bottles, joined by short Y tubes to the main tube in her arm.

"Hydration... and... what?" she muttered. The words came out as a mumble. She puckered her lips trying to force moisture forward from her throat.

Nick jumped from his chair. He had been dozing but was sentient enough to pour water and hold the straw to Leah's mouth. She drank with effort. When she spoke again, it was one word only.

"Nick?"

He seemed to be standing far above her. She struggled to focus, but the strain made her woozy.

"Pan!" She blurted with a force that surprised both Nick and the nurse who had just entered the room.

"That's a good sign," the nurse remarked blandly.

Nick held the pan to Leah's mouth and lifted her head from the pillow. She vomited and cried out in pain as the retching jostled her arm. The waves of nausea subsided and she lay back.

Nick wiped the edges of her mouth and raised the water to her lips once again, at the same time taking a second sputum cup from the bedside tray and holding it to her mouth.

"Spit the first sip out, and then I'll give you clean water to drink."

When she had drunk, Leah whispered, "What happened?"

Nick handed the pan to the nurse, who made a face as if it wasn't her job but his.

Anger overcame Nick's relief at hearing Leah speak.

"Someone shot you, that's what happened!"

"Shot me?"

"I'm angry at you, Leah! You're so damn stubborn. Don't you understand if we can't catch this guy he'll do what he needs to kill you. You can't keep going off to the vie cave; you've got to listen to me and the Lieutenant. You've got to!"

"Nick...I..."

Nick knew that as she struggled to speak her impulsive anger was filtering through the medication. Even now she would be defensive of her freedom.

He loved this feisty, independent spirit, and hated the way it catapulted her into serious trouble, not for the first time. Her erratic, quicksilver behavior had caused years of fear and grief. They lived as opposites in a wildly incompatible passion, her courage impetuous, his consistent, painstaking. Her work, spurts of intense energy; his constant, persistent.

"I'm sorry, Nick."

"I am too." He took her right hand and shook his head slowly, willing the angry words to mean that he wanted her safe, that he wanted to live with her the rest of his life, that he wanted her alive. "You've got to let it go, Leah. Whoever it is will kill you. He'll chase you down and kill you."

Before Leah could respond, the Lieutenant parted the curtains and came to stand by Nick.

"You are irresponsible, Leah."

Leah noted he'd used her first name.

"You cause me trouble I don't need. If Secondo hadn't found you, hadn't applied the tourniquet..."

"Secondo?" Her eyes popped wide.

He followed you this morning, not far behind, and when he heard the shot he ran and found you. He fashioned a tourniquet from a stick and part of his shirt. You're lucky, very lucky he was following. I don't understand why he was, but..."

"I remember. I saw him on the bench."

"In the car, bringing you to the hospital, Secondo told me he took the money you gave him and went to the little coffee shop near his house. Then he went on to the bar in the piazza and heard Sabina talking about you, so he knew you'd gone up the via cava." Nick said.

The Lieutenant broke in. "Given Sabina, everyone who drinks coffee in the morning knew you had been there early and gone up the trails. I'll be interviewing her."

"But everyone in town already knows I go up there."

The Lieutenant shook his head, frustrated. "And given Sabina, everyone who drinks coffee in the morning knew you had gone up there today. So it wouldn't be much for anyone willing to put their mind to it, to guess that since you're always up on the trails and you were up there today..."

"Okay, somebody's made a good guess that I saw Giulio being pushed off the cliff, but how could they know for certain? And anyway, I've seen other people on the trail."

"How many? Who?" He made a face.

"Okay, not many, but..."

"I didn't think so. Whoever was guessing, guessed correctly, unless there is some other reason, something you're not telling me, why someone would want to kill you."

Leah laughed, then winced in pain. "Was that a real question, Lieutenant? Did you find the bracelet?"

The Lieutenant's mouth dropped. "What bracelet?"

"I found a bracelet on table rock. A leather one with silver on it."

The Lieutenant looked at Secondo. "Did you find it?"

"There was no bracelet."

"That means the killer came to you after he shot you. *Mio Dio!*"

"He could have shot you again to make sure! He must have seen the blood and figured you'd bleed out soon anyway." Nick put his hands to his head.

"There must be some reason, some other reason why someone would want to kill me. It doesn't make sense that it would be just me seeing the murder, because anybody reasoning it through would know by now that I wasn't able to identify the murderer. What's another reason? Who even really knows me—enough to have any reason to kill me? And who cares if I write about the vie cave? They've been written about before, dozens of times. And that's all I'm doing here."

"Indeed, who really knows you?" The Lieutenant let the question hang in the air. "And writing about the vie cave is not all you're doing here. You're attentive, you're seeing things. You could be a threat. After Giulio's and then Signora Seta's death, I'm thinking the killer is probably in the throes of seriously twisted thinking. Something more than fear of discovery. Revenge for something?"

"Revenge for what?" Leah asked.

"I don't know." The Lieutenant shook his head. "I have to imagine all the possibilities. Stop and think. Since you've been here, working on this article, people are dying."

Leah turned her face to the wall. Without being aware of it, the Lieutenant could, if he persisted, convince her while she was in this vulnerable state, of being somehow responsible.

"Let me sleep. The murders have nothing to do with my article, but somehow everything to do with that cantina."

The Lieutenant hunched his shoulders, turned, and walked out through the slit in the curtains.

Leah opened her eyes and turned back to Nick. "Good riddance."

"Don't say it, Leah. He has to look from every side."

The nurse appeared, carrying a little paper cup with sleeping pills. Leah extended her good arm, took the glass of water from the nightstand, and swallowed the pills. Nick leaned to kiss Leah on the forehead. Then, picking up his book, he sat in the chair beside the bed. "Sleep, Leah. You need it."

Within minutes she was sleeping, immersed in the dark lake of her dreams.

Chapter Forty-Nine

The following morning Leah woke to find Nick still in the chair, watching her. "Have you been here all night?"

He waved his hand through the air as if to say 'of course'! "You've been restless. Still a lot of pain, right? I'm sorry."

"It'll get better soon."

A nurse appeared through the curtains and laid a syringe on the nightstand. "Of course it will get better."

When she put her hand on Leah's forehead, Leah shrank from her touch.

"Time for medication, Signora." She took the syringe from the tray and inserted it into the tube leading to Leah's arm.

"But I don't feel like I need more. It hurts, but not unbearably. Can't you wait?"

"Better to anticipate the pain, otherwise you'll have a very unpleasant catch-up."

"I think I can stand it."

The nurse gave her a condescending, smarmy smile as if she were addressing a little girl. "I'll decide. Remember, I'm the nurse."

When she stepped away, Leah turned to Nick and spoke in a loud whisper, "I don't like her. There's something funny about her."

As the words left her mouth, Leah noticed the nurse's feet below the curtain. She raised her index finger to her mouth, then pointed at the nurse's feet. In the silence, the nurse turned and tiptoed away.

An aide brought Leah's breakfast, and Nick smuggled in a croissant from the bar in the piazza to add to the distasteful gruel, but the morphine had dampened Leah's hunger. She nibbled without interest at the pastry and pushed the bowl of mush to the side.

"I can't figure this out. It made sense to chase me after the murder of Giulio, but why now? Surely the killer knows that if I had a picture, I would have given it to the police. How would killing me do any good? And if I didn't get a photo and didn't know who the murderer was—which if I had, would be common knowledge by now—then there's no need to kill me. Right?"

Nick smiled. Her speech was slow, drawn to inordinate length by the morphine.

"What's funny?"

"I'm sorry. I am listening and what you are saying makes sense. It's just I've never heard you speak so slowly. Maybe whoever it is just wants to kill you."

"Just because I'm me?"

"It just came into my mind; nothing else makes sense."

"Let's go over the possibilities again. There's got to be..."

"May we come in?" Anna's voice sounded from behind the curtain.

"Of course," Nick called, rising to his feet.

The Antoninis filed through the curtain and took turns embracing Leah and Nick.

"Leah," Anna's voice trembled with emotion. "We're so sorry. We knew the evening of the Befanata, something was wrong. I wish I'd encouraged you to speak more openly, maybe we could have prevented this."

"Please don't," Leah's voice trembled and her eyes were full of tears. "You couldn't have changed this, and I didn't want to add what I knew to the burden you already had with Giulio's death and the Befanata. Please don't feel badly."

The nurse appeared through the curtains. "Too many visitors! Shame on you!" She stared at the Antoninis and turned to Leah. "You need rest, Signora."

"Just a few more minutes, please. Then I'll go right to sleep."

"Five minutes. No more." The nurse left.

"She hovers over me like a mother duck."

Leonardo chuckled. "She's Giulio's distant cousin, didn't you know?"

"No one told me."

"She and Giulio were at odds about the inheritance, but I don't think she was ever a candidate."

"I'm more confused by the minute about all of this." Leah yawned. "Sorry."

"Don't apologize. We just wanted to say hello. We'll come back tomorrow."

When they had gone, Leah turned to Nick. "Do you think it's a coincidence that it's Giulio's cousin who's taking care of me? I mean could she have done it?"

"Don't let your imagination run away with you. The Antoninis would have alerted us if they felt anything was wrong with her, and they would know better than we do. Just get some sleep. I'm going for coffee, but I'll be back in a few minutes."

Chapter Fifty

Montaro stepped through the curtains surrounding Leah's bed. She was asleep. Nick, half asleep himself, sat up, startled to see Montaro.

Nick brought his fingers to his lips and in the same instant noticed Montaro held a large envelope. He whispered, "You got it enlarged?"

Montaro smiled. "I was going to show the Lieutenant. I thought he was here." He hugged the photo to his chest.

"He was here, but Leah was sleeping. I think he went for coffee. Can I see it?" Nick motioned toward the curtains. "We can step into the hallway."

Montaro followed but kept the photo close to his chest. They stopped outside the door.

"I'm sorry, but the Lieutenant must be the first one to see it. He'll be very angry if he isn't."

"Montaro we're in this up to our necks, and Leah's been shot for the whole business, whatever it is. She's the one suffering for it, so don't we have a right?" He reached for the photo.

Montaro drew back. "No! The Lieutenant is in charge. I'm sorry about your wife, Signor, but there are certain protocols. Still, you could come with me if you like. I'm sure we'll find him in the piazza."

Nick checked to make sure Leah was still sleeping, then rejoined Montaro, and the two set off down the steps.

"Could you see who it was?"

"After the Lieutenant, Signor."

They rushed out the back door of the hospital. It was market day; in the bright sun the piazza was crowded with late morning shoppers, some weighed with heavy bags of vegetables, fresh meat, brown-crusted Tuscan bread; others, housewives young and old, pulled their rolling carts slowly across the stone pavement of the piazza.

Nick and Montaro darted among them, brushing shoulders. A man carrying a heavy sack of groceries yelled after them, "Watch where you're going!"

Nick spotted the Lieutenant in the corner of the piazza near the main bar, talking to a group of older men who were sitting at a table in the sun, protected by a stone wall from the gentle but cold breeze.

As Nick approached the center of the piazza, he heard someone call, "Papa!"

A voice he knew. Nick jerked to a stop and swiveled around. Coming into the piazza from the far side, Sara and Jonathan were running toward him, Sara's arms outstretched for an embrace. Montaro veered to the right just in time to avoid colliding with Nick from behind.

"What are you doing here?" Nick yelled as they approached.

Sara stopped short, and Jonathan plowed into her from behind. Sara shrugged him off, straightened her jacket, and stomped her foot, yelling at Nick. "Fine welcome! I haven't seen you in months and you want to know what I'm doing here! I told you we were coming; I talked to Mom."

The absurdity of the situation struck Nick, and he laughed even as tears came to his eyes. Sara had stamped her foot the same way she had as a child. Montaro, who understood no English, was tugging at his sleeve motioning toward the Lieutenant; Leah was lying in a hospital bed, shot, the threat of death constantly over her head; and people had gathered to stare.

"Come here, Sara, Jonathan. I'm sorry." He spread his arms and clasped them in an embrace, whispering, "Listen, I have to speak fast, and you have to listen carefully and not talk. We're in a difficult situation, and I need you to follow my lead, no questions asked. Sara, your mom's okay, but she's been shot."

"Shot!!"

"Please don't make a show of it. It's an arm wound. She's fine, so keep calm. This man has important information, and we're taking it to the police lieutenant now." Nick nodded in the direction of the table where the Lieutenant and the old men were watching them. "So, come with me, don't say anything, and after, we'll see your mom."

"But where *is* Mamma?"

Nick touched her cheek, moved by Sara's use of 'Mamma,' the term she'd used as a little girl.

"She's in the hospital, and I'll take you there, but I must talk to the Lieutenant. And this," he turned to Montaro, "is Sergeant Montaro.

Sara opened her mouth to say something, but Nick jerked his open palms toward her and barked, "Not now, Sara! What your mother needs most is for us to identify the one who shot her. I'll explain later. Come on."

They rushed away across the piazza.

Jonathan held Sara's arm. "Listen to your dad. He said it's an arm wound and she's okay, so let's do as he says. He's got to deal with the police right now."

The men at the table had been watching them, amused by their shouts and what appeared to be an argument. Who was the young couple?

The Lieutenant knew and wondered why Montaro was standing there with them. He assumed it must be Leah and Nick's daughter and her fiancé. He walked to meet them.

Seeing the look on Nick's face, the Lieutenant pulled him aside. "What is it? Is she worse?"

Nick shook his head in answer and motioned toward the envelope Montaro held in his outstretched hand. The Lieutenant opened it. Nick leaned close. "My God! It looks like Italo!"

The Lieutenant held it close to his face, squinting.

Nick pointed, "The hat. Look at the hat. It's Italo's. I saw it in the back seat of his car and he was bragging about it. And the tassels. I saw them in his car. Who else has tassels like that? Or a hat that expensive?"

"Calm down, Signor. Many people have these cowboy hats."

"But not like this, not this expensive. And not with these tassels."

"These tassels are for sale. Anyone can buy them." The Lieutenant rubbed his chin. "We'd better find Italo. And you'd better tell me who these two are."

"My daughter, Sara, and her fiancé, Jonathan. A surprise visit."

Nick had ignored formal introductions, but the Lieutenant, imbued with centuries of the grace of his ancestors, extended his hand. "It's a pleasure to meet you both. I'm sorry it's in such circumstances."

Sara and Jonathan shook hands, both speaking at the same time, "Who's Italo?"

Secondo had come up behind them. "Are you looking for Italo? I just saw him going into the back entrance of the hospital."

"Oh, god!" Nick and the Lieutenant sprinted toward the hospital, the others trailing behind.

Chapter Fifty-One

Leah blinked her eyes. The drugs made her feel furry, thick-eyed. All she could see was a fuzzy outline standing at the foot of the bed. She rubbed her eyes and squinted.

The face came into focus.

"Wow! This is a surprise." A dull recollection of their uncomfortable interchange at the cenone flitted across her mind. "It's nice of you to come. I thought you'd left town after the Signora...."

"Was murdered? After we found her body? No. We didn't leave. We decided it was too late, too upsetting, so we stayed outside of town."

"How did you know I was here?"

"A little bird told me."

"A little bird? I don't understand." Leah's heart was pounding. She scooted against her pillows, and as she did, she noticed the bracelet.

"You!"

"Oh, this?" The killer raised an arm as if modeling the bracelet. "Yes, me, on the vie cave. Me on the trails above, along the ridge, trails you're too stupid to know anything about. And you're so smart! You know all about the vie cave, with your books and your cameras and your husband. Still, I was the one fooled! After I saw you bleeding on the trail, I was sure no one would find you in time. Then that idiot Secondo..."

"Nurse! Nurse!" Leah yelled.

"They're on report, sweetie pie. They won't hear you." Leah struggled to rise but was shoved back down.

"After I shot you, I bushwhacked a little way, dropped down to look at you, then back to the upper trail again to walk to the top. I got in my car on the far side of a field and headed back to town. Imagine how upset I was, coming down toward the bridge to see your dear, sweet little husband, that idiot Secondo, and the Lieutenant loading you into the car. But now..." Her voice turned to a deep singsong, "at the end of the game, Sweetie, everyone goes into the sack, the King—or shall I say the American—as well as the pawn."

"But..."

"Surprised?"

"Why? Why Giulio? Signora Seta? Me?"

"And you don't know it all."

"What?"

"Let's start with you. The photo. I could see the camera around your neck from the table rock. I thought maybe you knew who I was, but then when you obviously didn't, and when it seemed there was no photo, I figured I was safe. No, it wasn't you as a witness that bothered; it was your stupid flirting with Italo."

"I never flirted with Italo."

"The Befanata dance at the Antoninis?"

"That was..." Leah tried again to rise, jerking at the tube in her arms. Angelina shoved her down again.

"That was what *I* know it was! He's mine. I saw the way he looked at you and brought out a chair for you. You'll never have him!"

Leah gambled for time. "But Giulio and Signora Seta?"

"And that's not all! It's so funny, and you're so desperate to delay the inevitable! Like the others. Well, I like seeing you squirm. You and your pretty American life, with a mother and a father who probably never touched you. You don't know anything! You didn't know about Seta wanting to keep her precious cantina as it was. Italo deserved it, but that bitch messed it all up! When Giulio told me, I wanted to kill somebody." She laughed wildly. "And I did! I killed them all!" Angelina's eyes glittered with a strange lust.

Leah kicked out, striking Angelina in the side, but Angelina pushed her back and reached for the pillow.

Gasping in pain, Leah struck her in the face with her right fist, but her strength was dampened by morphine, and Angelina laughed as the light blow slid off her jaw.

"It won't take long, bitch. Carry this thought with you: Giulio, his aunt… all of it is a long tale of love, more love than you could ever dream of or understand. And an interfering wench like yourself doesn't deserve an explanation."

She reverted to a sickly-sweet voice. "Take it like a woman, sweetie. I have, for my whole life. And I won't anymore. The bell has sounded. The murders have just begun."

"Like hell…"

Leah meant the words to be strong, but they stumbled from her lips, and Angelina pushed her down, pressing the pillow over her face. With a muffled cry of pain, Leah batted at it, but her arm was moving through molasses. She smelled the clean lemon scent of the laundry soap, even as she struck ever more weakly at the air, and finally knew only darkness.

Chapter Fifty-Two

Nick and the Lieutenant burst through the doorway of Leah's room and yanked open the curtains. Seeing the figure at the bed, they grasped her by the arms and flung her back, away from Leah.

Angelina screamed, "Don't touch me! Get off me! Get off!" It was a scream she knew by heart.

Sara darted to grab the pillow from her mother's face. "Mamma! Mamma!" She leaned close, holding her cheek next to her mother's mouth to feel her breath.

Jonathan, seeing Leah motionless and pale, felt certain she was gone. He tried to calm Sara. "Sara, the nurse is coming. It's okay. It's okay."

Quivering with fury, Angelina fought to break free. The Lieutenant and Nick struggled against her surprising strength.

"It's Italo's, you stupid, stupid fools! He wants it! You don't know anything! He wants it."

They compelled her toward the doorway. Two nurses rushed past them, shouting for Sara and Jonathan to move out of the way.

In the hallway, Montaro cuffed Angelina, and he and the Lieutenant led her away. Nick could hear her screaming, "Damn you, bastards. All of you!"

Chapter Fifty-Three

With quick, precise movements, the older nurse bent over Leah and slipped her fingers to the side of Leah's neck, searching for a heartbeat. "Barrier," she said quietly to the other nurse, who quickly pulled open the drawer on the bed stand and drew out a plastic sheet with a cloth webbing in the center of it.

While the older woman gave mouth to mouth and compressions, the younger raced out and came back with a defibrillator. The current jolted Leah's body again and then again.

With a cough and cry, she started up and then fell back moaning.

"Mamma!" Sara stepped toward the bed, but the nurse pushed her away. "Let her come back. She needs to figure out where she is, what's happened."

At the sound of Sara's voice, Leah opened her eyes. Confused, she stared at her daughter. "Sara?"

Back in the room, Nick nudged against the nurse and leaned over Leah. He tried to speak, but his voice broke. He bent to kiss her forehead.

"She's okay, Papa. She's okay."

Leah smiled at them. "It was Angelina. And now here are Sara and Jonathan. I don't understand."

"Don't try, Mamma. Rest and get well."

"This wasn't the way I imagined it. I thought we'd go to Rome to get you." Leah's words came slowly. Her eyes were glazed and she strained to keep them open. She ran her tongue over her lips.

"We'll figure it out later, Leah. Just rest. Please." Nick brushed her cheek with the back of his hand.

"Yes!" the older nurse agreed with a snort. "And you all need to leave so she *can* rest."

"No," Nick glared at the nurse. "I'm not leaving."

"Would you like me to call the Lieutenant back again and make another scene to upset your wife all the more?"

"Of course not! But I'm her husband!"

"And I'm her nurse!"

Chapter Fifty-Four

Italo sat on the edge of his chair in front of Lieutenant Cavour's desk. "She asked to borrow it. She said wearing my clothes...." He hesitated, fumbling with the edge of his jacket. "...turned her on."

"Turned her on?" The Lieutenant opened both palms.

"You know, a rush," Italo responded, abashed.

"No, I don't know. Why don't you tell me?"

"She was always doin' it...wearing my shirts when we were alone, that sort of thing. And I thought the hat was just the same thing. I swear to you, I didn't know anything about the other." His face took on a horrified look. "Wait a minute! Do you think she did it on purpose to implicate *me*?"

The Lieutenant smiled. "I don't know, Italo. But it seems improbable you didn't know what she was planning. You're intimate with her, you spend plenty of time with her by all accounts, you travel with her. She must have given hints."

"She's crazy, I'm telling you. She's obsessed with me and always doing weird stuff like wearing my clothes. Like I was a king or something. But she's nuts. She even calls me 'Daddy' sometimes."

If Italo thought he was proving his distance and innocence, he was wrong. The Lieutenant responded, "And you like that sort of thing I suppose?"

Italo grinned. "Well, yeah, sort of..." and then thinking better of what he was saying, "I mean no, not that part, not that part."

The Lieutenant shook his head. "And what does your wife think of Angelina's obsessions and your acquiescence to it?"

Italo's head jerked up. "I didn't know you knew I was married. You won't

176

tell her...."

"Are you so naïve? It's the business of the police to know things, and we know much more than most people think. In fact, what I'm saying is true in general. You should have learned by now that women are more observant than men. You can tell yourself your wife didn't know, but she did. I think I can positively say that Angelina and your wife knew about each other for a long time, and you will learn that lesson in the most unexpected way, I'm sure."

He let it sink in. "You told Nick that your wife knew about Angelina and was fine with it."

Italo blushed. "I was bragging a little."

"I see..."

"Please don't tell her, please."

"You weren't listening. I don't need to tell her."

"But she's said nothing."

"She's biding her time. At any rate, we are releasing full details of the case to the press this afternoon, so everything will be on the news and in the papers. And of course, we'll be checking your alibis, so word will get around. The whole region will be buzzing."

"But my hat is such a little part of it. Do you have to mention that?"

"When the louse falls into the hopper, he thinks, for a while anyway, to be the miller."

"I know, but why do you have to tell?"

"Tiburzi the Second cowed by his wife? Buck up, Italo, the word is already out. You've been with Angelina a long time and you would have to be particularly naïve to think no one understood your relationship."

"But I only presented her as a friend."

"Italo, Italo..." The Lieutenant shook his head. "Sometimes I am ashamed to be of the male gender. We can be so stupid in our egotism. I think the best thing you can do is to get the jump on asking forgiveness by buying some very fine presents. And I mean diamonds, not chocolates."

The Lieutenant laughed, but suddenly turned serious. "And, Italo, think hard about all this. Your ego has gotten the better of you. Worse than having an affair is having taken advantage of a very troubled woman, you know what I mean. Her father. She's a woman so desperate after years of abuse that she would kill to make you happy – to make the only man she thought really loved her happy. And you used her."

Italo rushed out of Cavour's office, glancing backward, as if the Lieutenant might be following. Rounding the corner, he slammed head-on into Nick, who had just stepped forward to open the door for Leah. Nick fell against her, and she screeched at the blow to her arm.

"What the hell are you doing, Italo!" Nick shoved him away and turned to Leah, who was wincing in pain.

"Sorry, I didn't mean to…" He rushed off into the street.

Leah cradled her arm in the palm of her hand.

"Are you okay?"

"What a donkey that guy is!"

"I'm sorry about your arm." Nick made a funny face. "But he did apologize."

Leah laughed, "Okay, okay. But as the saying goes, the 'appetite of his ego exceeds the grocery store of my soul.' And I won't be sad when the news hits the stands and televisions. It's funny to think how his wife will shred him, but it isn't funny to think of Angelina's childhood or the savagery of her love. Maybe if he'd left her alone…"

Inside the station, the secretary, bright red hair bobbing above a tight, bright blue sweater, short black skirt, and thigh-high black boots, opened the Lieutenant's door for Nick and Leah. The Lieutenant came around his desk to greet them.

"You're smiling. You must have run into Italo. He left in a great hurry, on his way to the jeweler's, I think." A sly smile creased his dark, handsome face. He motioned them to the chairs in front of his desk and took his own seat.

"Thanks for seeing us, Lieutenant, we wanted to find out what's going to happen now."

"I'm glad to see you both, Leah. It's been a trying, intense time and there are things you need to know. Once we finish the paperwork, it will all go to the office of the District Judge. He will issue orders to decide whether or not Angelina is competent to be tried. A psychiatric evaluation. I think you know by now, there's her history to consider. If she's found fit, she may be offered a fast-track trial."

"What's that?" Nick and Leah asked in unison.

"I think you don't have it in America. I don't know." He put his hand to his forehead. "Anyway, it limits the number of witnesses and the kind of evidence that can be submitted, and if she's convicted, then it gives her only two-thirds of the usual sentence. And all the proceedings of a fast-track trial are closed to the public."

"Her father will want that." Leah spat the words. "If she doesn't take the fast-track?"

"It could be months before she's indicted, and after that, it could more months."

Nick grunted. "But we can't stay for months and months."

"You won't be expected to. We'll keep you informed, and you'll come back."

"What if we can't?" said Nick.

The Lieutenant smiled warmly. "You must! And do you really imagine you won't come back? I think even with our troubles, you won't stay away. And remember, technically, neither Angelina nor Italo are from here. They are not Scansansianese."

"I'm not sure that helps." Leah shook her head. "But it doesn't matter, because you're right, even murder wouldn't keep us away."

Nick looked at her, eyebrows raised.

Leah went on. "But I have more questions. Was it Italo's rifle, and what will happen to the cantina? Angelina said something about a meeting."

"It's very important to us that it's no one from here, Leah. If it were, it would be like discovering someone in the family was a killer. As for the rifle, yes, it was Italo's. He was carrying it in his car without permission, so Angelina had it with her when she borrowed the car the day she shot you. As for the cantina, there's more to that story. I'll fill you in later, but I imagine now it will be Andrea's, and it's bound to be a long bureaucratic process. We should know by the time you get back." He smiled. "Whatever happens, I have your contact information and I'll be in touch with you. For now, I hope you can rest. You'll need to be planning for the wedding, yes? And Nick, you should know that people here appreciate your work. They're excited you appreciate the old traditions. And you..." he turned to Leah, "they think you're brave, although I would call it something else."

Chapter Fifty-Five

The day of the wedding dawned cold and overcast but turned warm and sunny by noon. In the high-ceilinged foyer of the theater, just off the piazza, long tables were covered with crisp white linen and laden with local wines. Sweets, breads, braided mozzarella cheeses with tomatoes, Saturnella, gorgonzola, octopus and grilled sardines, salamis, wide bowls of green salads, heaping trays of bananas, tangerines, and kiwi, trenchers of roasted lamb and grilled chicken, olives, marinated chickpeas, and tray after tray of cakes, biscotti, and chocolate custard tarts. The wedding cake, a custard fruit torte three feet across, sat in the middle of it all.

Dressed in smaller versions of their parents' dark three-piece suits and colorful knit dresses, boys and girls chased each other back and forth. They screamed and swooped by the tables to grab biscotti on the run, like gulls after bread. The adults milled around the room laughing, chatting, moving to the table to refill their plates, turning back again to greet friends they hadn't seen since autumn. The whole town came.

Lieutenant Cavour approached Leah and extended his hand. "A fine thing, no? You can feel the sense of renewed joy, and of relief that the other is over. How's the arm?"

Leah smiled. "Joy yes, and on my part, surprise. You told me the bureaucracies here move slowly, but it seemed we got the wedding together in an impossibly short time. Everyone has been so helpful."

The Lieutenant nodded. "And the arm?"

"Much better. It will take a while, but I think there's improvement every day."

The Lieutenant patted her shoulder gently. Since the shooting, the two had developed a mutual, easy respect for each other.

Leah went on. "We have you and many others to thank: the mayor, the provincial office, which I think was also your doing, Lieutenant, and Signor Scarpa here at the city office, which I think was also your doing, and the civil registrar, which as well may have been your doing. If bureaucracies move slowly, I think that's not the case when you're in charge." Leah laughed.

"I didn't have *that* much to do with it."

"Don't deny it. I know how things work—or don't. And we appreciate it. Plus Maria at the flower shop, Sabina at the bar, Andrea and Silvio for the music, Giovanna for the wedding favors, the Signorine Marini at the restaurant, and more than I can say, the Antoninis."

"The Antoninis, yes. They do more for this town than you can imagine. You're fortunate to know them. They are as good as bread."

Leah nodded and fell silent, thinking of her friends. "But what I can't figure out is how Sara and Jonathan did it all."

The Lieutenant grinned. "It was easy—well, fairly easy."

As if summoned, Sara and Jonathan appeared one on each side of Leah and reached in turn to shake the Lieutenant's hand.

"You look radiant!" The Lieutenant said, his full attention on Sara. Suddenly embarrassed by his enthusiasm, he turned to Jonathan. "And I'll concede you are looking very trim as well, though I am the more handsome." He winked at Sara, took her hand, and kissed it.

Sara faced Jonathan, "Well, Lieutenant, you certainly are among the most handsome of men, but I think Jonathan may just have the edge." She put her hand to Jonathan's cheek.

Cavour's smile reflected nostalgia.

Leah took note. "But how did you two arrange it all so quickly?"

Sara winked at the Lieutenant. "Don't be shy, Lieutenant. You helped us, and that's why it got done. But there's another reason as well. We weren't in Prague when we called. We were in Florence at the U.S. Consulate General. We had already been to the Consulate General of Italy in San Francisco before we came, which was, I have to tell you, manned by a very uncooperative clerk."

The Lieutenant laughed aloud. "Never in?"

"Not only never in; never returned calls, and when he did have the information we needed, he didn't let us know. Anyway, once we'd slogged through that, the going was fairly easy. The U.S. Consulate was nonchalant and signed papers with barely a glance."

"I'm sorry about the mix-up with the registrar. I didn't know he was out of town, but he was kind enough to cut short his time in Rome."

"Don't worry Lieutenant. All's well that ends well. He was perfect, even if Jonathan and I didn't understand everything. And the way Don Eduardo fixed the bells! They must have rung for a half hour!"

"By the way, I need to talk to you both tomorrow. Can you come into the office in the afternoon?"

"What's it about?" Leah and Nick spoke at once.

"I want to share some information with you, but not now, not here at the wedding."

"Uh, okay," Leah could see the warning in the Lieutenant's eyes and turned to Sara to change the subject.

"Sara, what about the U.S. guests, all those invitations?"

"I hadn't sent them yet." She hugged her mother. "Only a few, so it was no problem, and we'll have a reception when we get back. How could we have passed up an Italian wedding when you two were here? It was our only chance."

Chapter Fifty-Six

"I didn't want to spoil the wedding with more sad news. But I think you need to know there was a third murder."

"My god! Who?" Nick jumped to his feet.

"It's no one you knew, Nick, and not from Scansansiano. But connected." He turned to Leah. "I'm guessing by the fact you didn't respond to my news, you anticipated what I have to say?"

"She killed her father."

It was the Lieutenant's turn to be surprised. "What made you think that?"

"A guess. I had inklings at the cenone that she was having delusions about Italo and me. Weird suspicions and hints about how I didn't know the real world. Then in the hospital room, it was clear. And I'd heard about the abuse."

"Well, you're right. I think when Giulio told her, on table rock, about Andrea and Giulio's meeting with Signora Seta it was too much. For her, Italo getting the cantina for a restaurant was her ticket away from her father and a firmer tie to Italo. But Signora Seta had stopped wavering and decided to keep the cantina as a cantina. Angelina killed Giulio half by accident in the shock of that news, I think. But circumstances snowballed. She failed to get you, and in her heightened state, she went after Signora Seta. Italo was the only 'stable' thing in her life, and in some way, she thought she was protecting him and his interests, and she needed to keep him, not lose him to some foreign woman. I think she had a psychotic break, and her father, after all these years of abuse, got caught up in it all. Who can follow her reasoning?"

"But when did she kill him?" Leah asked.

"After Signora Seta. My guess is she went home to get something, probably in a confused, heightened state of mind, and he started in on her. From what others say now that he's dead—the cowards, none of them intervened—it was all gossip and she wouldn't press charges. But he'd been raping her since she was five years old and had taught her she was to be available whenever he wanted. So when she got there, jacked-up from having just killed someone else, she snapped and ended the torment of the abuse."

Leah's eyes welled with tears, "What will happen to her?"

"I don't know for sure, but I imagine her lawyer will enter a guilty by reason of insanity plea and she'll be institutionalized."

Nick said, "I don't blame her for killing her father."

"Why wasn't it in the news?"

"We came to a polite agreement with the local media. There are some complications."

"What about Andrea? Why didn't he say anything?"

"He was sure it implicated him. He'll be charged."

The three of them fell silent.

Chapter Fifty-Seven

Giovanna entered the dingy hallway, followed by the guard, who dangled keys in his hand. They passed three empty cells. In the fourth, behind a glass barrier, Angelina was alone, sitting on a chair, hands in her lap, staring at the doorway. When she heard the key in the lock, Angelina tilted her head to the side. "It's you."

"Who else?" Giovanna stepped into the room with a glance back at the guard, who had retreated to stand beside the door.

Angelina's short-sleeved, baggy gray dress hung loosely on her thin frame. Wan and bleary-eyed, she stared at Giovanna as if she weren't sure of who she was.

Giovanna shivered in the cold, still air of the visiting room, wondering if Angelina didn't feel the cold, or if the jail didn't provide sweaters.

"So?" Angelina's voice grated the air.

"Nothing." Giovanna shrugged.

"What are you doing here?"

"I came to see you."

"Why?"

"I don't know." She looked around the bare room, and back into Angelina's eyes. "I'm glad Giulio's dead, and I'm glad your father's dead."

"Yeah? Well, I wish you'd have killed them instead of me. Then I wouldn't be here."

They both emitted a desultory laugh, but Giovanna felt a tremor of fear up her back. "You need anything?"

"What do you think! I need Italo and some decent clothes, and food. *Mio*

Dio! the swill they give us."

"Clothes I can bring. Shampoo? Soap?"

"Are you saying I smell, I'm dirty?"

"No! I'm just trying to help."

"I didn't mean to do it, not really, but they won't believe me. I wanted Italo to have the cantina. For the restaurant. We're going to make a restaurant."

Giovanna cringed. Italo had scurried back to his wife, tail between his legs. She didn't say.

"But why up the via cave?"

"Early morning. No one around. We could talk. I wanted him to get things moving."

"Except Contarini…"

"That bitch! If I ever get outa here…"

Giovanna scooted back. "But Signora Seta?"

Angelina sniffed and wiped her arm across her nose. "Same thing. I wanted her to give Italo a chance, but she wouldn't. She wanted it to stay a cantina."

Her speech had become pressured like a steam roller moving inexorably forward, smashing all in front of it. "But the one I wish I had killed is that bitch of an American, Contarini."

"She wasn't after Italo. It was a coincidence."

"Don't listen to that shit. She was after Italo. Flirting. Damn foreign women come here ready for a fling so they can write their damn books and articles about love in Italy. God, I'd like to get my hands on her. And hey, what about my dad! You like that? You were always saying I should leave him."

Angelina's voice had risen and she beat the bed with each staccato word. The guard moved toward them.

"Guard, I'm ready to go," Giovanna shouted.

Angelina banged on the glass. Her face had become blotched with red spots. "Don't go! Please! Don't go! Stay and talk."

Giovanna stepped away. "I've got to get back to work. I'm helping Silvio in the shop."

Angelina struck the glass. "Bitch! You're all the same! When I get out you'll all see!"

The door clanged shut.

Chapter Fifty-Eight

Leah and Nick were relaxing with a cup of tea before packing the last box of books to be shipped to the U.S.

"Overall it's been good, hasn't it?" She brushed her fingers across his hand.

"Only you could say that after being chased by a murderer, getting shot, finding dead bodies..."

"All that, yes, but we also got our work done, finally. The article's in, if late, and you're bound to get a raise and relief from 'the process.'"

Leah waited a few minutes before going on.

"Nick?"

"Yeah?"

"I got a letter from *Get Up and Go!*

"And they're paying you an extra $5000 because the article was so good."

"I wish."

"Then what?"

"They want me to do another piece."

"On?"

"My choice. I'm still thinking."

"This year?"

"Next."

"So we'll come back. I'll teach summer and take fall. That is if you're getting paid well."

"They've offered airfare and twice as much for the article."

"It's a deal. Just no more murders, okay?"

Leah tossed her head, laughing, "Don't be ridiculous! Two, or three—and a half—happening at once in such a small town will be a record for a hundred years."

Acknowledgements

Many people have a hand in making a book. I cannot thank all of them here, but I would like to express gratitude to at least some.

Most particularly I want to thank my husband and children. Steve, for the many mornings over coffee when he not only put off his own work to listen to, critique, and augment my ideas with his scholarly knowledge and incisive mind, but also read the drafts of the book, aiding me at every turn by his editorial expertise. All of my sons, Dov z"l,Lev, and Gidon, deserve deep thanks for the myriad ways they encourage and support. All four of these men, by their courage, indomitable spirit, and love of life have given me more than storyteller can tell or pen can write.

For many years, my Italian friends have renewed and sustained me in community and friendship. The books are mysteries, but at the heart I hope the reader will find a sense of community and love of life. I thank Pino Zennaro, Annalisa Longo, Lorenzo Zennaro, Gianni D'Este Widmann, Umberto Sartori, Angela Pampanini, Roberto Nizzi, Martina Nizzi, and acknowledge in memory Bruno Nizzi, Filomena Travagli, and Elise Brugi, all of whom cared for, housed, fed, laughed, and cried with me and my family for decades. Thanks to Carlo Fè, whose photography is a gift to Tuscany and all who see it and to Luigi Cerroni who gave generously of his time and knowledge of the *vie cave*, fed us homemade pasta chitarra, and introduced us to the Befanata. .

I want to give thanks as well to my friends: Carol McNamara, political theorist extraordinaire and friend; Roz Stein, master educator and sister-in-law; Pamela Lazarus, who opened the door to in-the-field experiences I could not have had without her help; and Mary and Steve Sharp, the best of U.S. neighbors.All of these generous people read and helped improve my work.

Finally, I want to thank Harriette Sackler, Agatha Award-Nominated Short Story Writer and co-publisher and editor of Level Best Books, a woman of generosity, compassion, and astute observation, who has helped me become a better storyteller.

About the Author

Libi Siporin has spent her life traveling and writing. As in her other books, her mysteries arise from experiences of life and work in Niger, West Africa; Afghanistan; Italy; the U.S.; and Israel. Siporin prefers to face forward and move in high gear, preferably outdoors. When she does stop to look behind her, she finds two great mentors accompanying her: love and death. *Bitter Maremma* is the first of the Leah Contarini Mysteries.